UNWILLING MISTRESS

UNWILLING MISTRESS

BY

LINDSAY ARMSTRONG

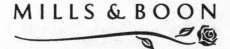

MILLS & BOON LIMITED
ETON HOUSE, 18–24 PARADISE ROAD
RICHMOND, SURREY TW9 1SR

First published in Great Britain 1993
by Mills & Boon Limited

© Lindsay Armstrong 1993

Australian copyright 1993
Philippine copyright 1993
Large Print edition 1994

ISBN 0 263 13773 2

Set in Times Roman 16 on 17½ pt.
16-9404-53463 C

Printed and bound in Great Britain by
Mackays of Chatham PLC, Chatham, Kent

CHAPTER ONE

'AND this is the Ballroom Forest I was telling you about. As you can see there are wonderful examples of myrtle, sassafras and King Billy pines—and when you've seen enough we'll go back to that little beach on Lake Dove and take a break,' Briony Richards said to her little band of hikers, all but one of whom were over sixty and a party of Americans travelling together.

'This is just something!' Dwight Weinberg from Chicago enthused. 'Dora, can you believe these trees?' he added to his wife as his video camera whirred.

'And the shade and the waterfall!' Dora called back. 'My oh, my!'

Briony smiled faintly and took off her hat. She was twenty-seven, tall and her hair tumbled down to her shoulders in a cloud of sun-streaked curls. Her eyes were a steady blue, her skin smooth and tanned and the sleeveless khaki top and shorts she wore with climbing boots and thick socks showed off long legs and a trim, well-proportioned figure. She was also used to the effect the beautiful Cradle Mountain region of Tasmania had on visitors, although it never failed to give her a bit of a glow.

But as she sat down on a smooth boulder beside the waterfall it occurred to her that one member of the party, a man and the only other one apart from her below sixty, was not as enthusiastic as the rest, at least not for the mountain or forest scenery. In fact it seemed that more often his gaze was on her and, as she looked up, it was straight into a pair of enigmatic hazel eyes. Damn him, she thought as she looked away coolly. He's obviously going to be one of *those*. What on earth is a man like that doing here on his own, anyway? And why isn't he climbing Marions Lookout instead of trailing along on a soft walk like this? she thought scornfully, then bit her lip. Because in among her scorn was the tacit acknowledgement that Grant Goodman, and all she knew about him was his name, was some specimen of manhood. At least six feet four, she judged, as strong as a lion by the look of it yet light-footed and agile, and with similar tawny colouring.

She'd met him for the first time the previous evening, in her capacity as manager of Heath House, an Alpine lodge in the area. After dinner actually was when he'd first come to her notice. A group of guests had prevailed upon her to play the wonderful old pianola and they'd got quite into the party spirit. Not that she could have accused Grant Goodman of that, precisely. He had nursed a solitary drink in front of the huge log fire and sat on the sidelines so to speak. But he'd nevertheless contrived to make her conscious of his gaze on her from time to time, and peculiarly conscious that she looked well in her long-sleeved, wine-red dress that accentuated her bust and slender waist and showed off her legs admirably.

It had been a slightly unnerving sensation because she'd actually dressed hastily and with no plan to fix anyone's attention, yet here was this man making her feel as if she'd dressed solely with him in mind... And contriving to make her wonder who he was, why he was alone—and why he should be making such an impression on her so that her pumping of the pedals was a trifle erratic. Then he'd got up and left quietly and not one woman in the party, be they sixty or otherwise, had been able to control the involuntary glance in his direction. Damn him, she thought again.

Her confused musings were interrupted by the party's deciding they had seen enough and she led them back to the beach where everyone took off their backpacks and pulled out their refreshments.

Dwight Weinberg came to squat beside Briony. The Weinbergs and the two other couples travelling together were on a round-the-world trip on a scale that made Briony feel exhausted just to contemplate it, but in the two days they'd spent so far at Heath House she'd come to like them all. Also to realise that they were endlessly curious, as Dwight proceeded to demonstrate.

'You Aussies can turn your hand to any-thing, can't you, Briony?' he said admiringly. 'Take yourself—you manage the lodge, you're a mountain guide and a veritable fount of knowledge. I take my hat off to you!'

Briony stared out over the deep blue waters of Lake Dove then briefly up to the twin peaks of Cradle Mountain before she replied. 'I'm not usually the guide, Dwight,' she said wryly. 'He's sick today, that's why you've got me.'

'But you can do it!' Dwight persisted.

'And do it so well,' her five other sexagenarians chorused, nodding their grey heads.

She smiled round affectionately. 'You're very kind. I just hope,' she said with a teasing glint, 'you'll all go away and spread the word about Heath House.'

'We will but it's sure going to be hard to tear ourselves away!' Dwight responded. 'Tell me something, though, Briony—although your resort is only a year old, I believe it's just been sold?'

Briony grimaced inwardly and wondered how Dwight had picked that bit of information up. 'It's not mine, Dwight, I only work there, but yes, it's due to change hands very shortly although we've been more or less assured that everything will go on the same.'

'Good,' Dwight said briskly. 'When you're on to a good thing stick to it, I always say, and made myself a mint doing just that,' he added proudly. 'And I would also say you're the best thing that ever happened to Heath House.'

For some reason, and perhaps it was because he had taken no part in this admiration session, Briony looked up and straight into

Grant Goodman's hazel eyes. He'd stripped off his backpack and was holding a can of soft drink to his lips, but what surprised her was the look of considerable irony she encountered as their gazes met. She narrowed her own eyes and was sufficiently surprised to be unable to look away for a moment. Then he lowered the can and the irony was gone, to be replaced by cool amusement, causing Briony to think as she turned away at last, Who the hell *is* he and why should he look at me like that?

It was not something she was able to answer as she led the party back to the Lake Dove car park, and she was annoyed to find it irking her as she tried to concentrate on describing the Alpine scenery, identifying the wild flowers for them and just doing something she always enjoyed on a rare perfect day in the area beneath a cloudless sky. And she chided herself, as she strode along and breathed in the scent of lemon thyme and scanned the beautiful lake cupped below rugged peaks, for bothering her head with it at all. She was used to handling men who tried to take all kinds of liberties, she assured herself, and ignored the slight mental tremor she experienced. One did not rise in the hospitality trade unless one was adept at dealing with all sorts of passes and all sorts of men on the loose. But the fact remained that there was something about this one that did bother her.

And it was no comfort, when they got back to the Heath House minibus, to see him end up sitting beside the driver's seat while the rest of the party arranged themselves in pairs behind, as they fanned themselves, caught their breath and chattered away about the sheer beauty and magnificence of Cradle Mountain—and craned their necks for a last look as she drove the bus away.

'You drive well, Briony—may I call you that?' Grant Goodman remarked, as she changed gear and negotiated the narrow, winding road.

'Certainly, Mr Goodman,' she replied brightly although inwardly clenching her teeth, in a manner of speaking.

'Grant,' he murmured with a faint idle smile on his lips. 'You also handle people well.'

'Oh, I don't know. *Most* people are pretty easy to get along with,' she said flatly.

There was a moment's silence then he said reflectively, 'It annoys you that I should make these comments—I wonder why?'

Briony compressed her lips on the hot retort that sprang to them and could have killed herself for allowing her prejudice to show through—also for feeling somewhat unnerved as he sat so easily beside her, his long, jean-clad legs a little cramped so that their knees were almost touching. He had his arms folded and out of the corner of her eye she could see the golden hairs on them and one hand that was strong but well-shaped.

'No reason, Mr Goodman,' she said then and decided to take another line. 'What brings you to Cradle Mountain?'

He took a moment to respond and shrugged slightly. 'One hears so much about Tasmania's wilderness areas, doesn't one?'

'One does,' she agreed. 'So you're from the mainland?'

'Yes,' he said, and added obligingly, 'Sydney, to be precise, Briony, and I'm here to rest and recharge the batteries as well as take in the wonders of the scenery. I do hope you don't object.'

He spoke well, she thought, and his voice was light-timbred and could be fascinating... She wrenched her mind away. 'Why should I? I——'

'I just thought you had taken a slight dislike to me,' he drawled, and as she switched her gaze to his for a moment he smiled at her in a way that was intimate, amused and lazily insolent.

Briony turned her attention back to the road and changed gear viciously. 'Not at all, Mr Goodman,' she retorted crisply. 'A guest is a guest; we place a high priority on service at Heath House and we believe in making them all welcome.'

'I'm relieved to hear you say so,' he murmured, and added, 'One wonders how welcome.'

'What do you mean?'

'Well, were I to tell you that you have—uh—somewhat taken my fancy, would *that* service be included?'

Briony gasped and swerved a little wildly to miss nothing. 'I don't believe you,' she said through her teeth.

'That's no reason to try to wipe me off the face of the earth in the wilds of Tasmania,' he said with a grin as she straightened the bus.

'I wish I *could* —— ' She stopped abruptly and swallowed.

'Everything all right, Briony?' Dwight called.

'Fine! Sorry about that, folks,' she called back. 'Some sort of slimy reptile gave me a bit of a fright,' she added.

Grant Goodman had even, very white teeth against his tan and he laughed silently but with genuine appreciation. He also said mildly, 'I don't suppose it would look too good on one of those inevitable questionnaires hotels are always so keen to have you fill out that the manager called you a slimy reptile.'

'Ah, but that is one of the advantages of being a manager,' she shot back. 'They come to me anyway.'

He considered, still looking amused. 'Of course,' he said eventually. 'You know, you're good with your fists—speaking metaphorically. I like that too. I once had a mare rather like you, by the way. She was mettlesome and spirited, had lovely lines—and required a strong hand to keep her in order sometimes,' he said dispassionately.

Briony actually felt herself swelling with rage, an unpleasant sensation but she couldn't remember being more angry in her life, and it was just as well her fists were full of steering-wheel and that the gates of Heath House were upon them because for an awful moment she was tempted to try to punch Grant Goodman on the mouth.

'Wise,' he said gently, as she brought the minibus to a less than smooth stop.

'Mr Goodman,' she said precisely, barely audibly and with a white shade around her mouth, 'I don't have to put up with this and if there's any more of it I shall have to ask you to leave Heath House.'

His lips twisted. 'You could always try, Briony, although I'm not quite sure under what charge, but be that as it may—this image you're presenting me with at the moment doesn't quite sit with what I've heard about you,' he said musingly.

Briony stared at him, her eyes wide and stunned, her nostrils flaring, her lips parted. Then she whispered, 'Get out, damn you, before I do hit you!'

He raised an eyebrow and smiled slightly. 'By all means,' he returned pleasantly. 'I hope I haven't ruined your day but I'm staying for a week so perhaps I'll be able to put things between us on a more—conciliatory footing. See you at dinner,' he added, unwinding his long legs and stepping leisurely out of the bus.

Briony was still shaking inwardly by the time she reached the sanctity of her own quarters.

Heath House had been architecturally designed to blend in with the Alpine scenery. A mixture of stone and timber, the central house contained the dining-rooms and lounges, kitchen, reception and the manager's suite. There were huge fireplaces, wide verandas and all the main rooms were panelled with a variety of Tasmanian timber such as blackwood and sassafras. There were deep settees, lovely rugs on the polished floors and wonderful arrangements of dried flowers. It was both comfortable and stunning. The guests, maximum forty, were accommodated in individual chalets scattered about the main complex, which were luxurious and spacious, all with their own woodburning stoves and spa baths. And the whole complex sat in a lovely, mountainous woodland setting that came alive at night with native creatures such as possums and pademelons, quolls, wombats and Tasmanian devils.

The architectural foresight that had seen Heath House blend so beautifully with its surroundings extended to the manager's quarters. Briony had a bedroom, sitting-room, kitchenette and her own spa bath all situated behind the reception area, and all very private.

And it was straight to the spa that she took her quivering senses and outraged spirit. But even the warm, bubbling water and mass-aging jets failed to make her feel better and it was rather grimly that she dried herself and started to dress. Dinner was only an hour and a half away and in keeping with the spirit of Heath House, small and exclusive number-wise, she or a deputy always dined with the guests, and steered the evening towards pleasant conviviality for those who wanted it.

She padded from her spa bathroom to her bedroom and opened her built-in wardrobe. It was still warm and gave promise of being a cloud-free, balmy evening. But as she stared at the rack of clothes she wasn't seeing them.

Instead, lodged in her mind's eye was a re-run of the events that had seen her virtually bury herself and her talents in the wilds of Tasmania. And she closed her eyes in sudden pain, and wondered dully when the pain would end—not while there were men around like Grant Goodman, who had somehow got hold of the story, she thought. But how? And had he simply recognised the name and put two and two together? What an awful co-incidence, she mused starkly, but surely it couldn't be any more than that?

She came out of her reverie with a sigh and applied herself to getting dressed. She chose a loose blue linen smock that matched her eyes, had some intricate silver thread em-broidery down the front, and gave only a hint of her figure beneath it. She slid her feet into silver flatties and brushed her hair back and tied it loosely. But as she stared at herself in her dressing-table mirror she made a dis-covery that astounded her. For over twelve months she'd battened down on every vestige of sensuality in her nature. She'd worked un-ceasingly on getting Heath House off the ground and running and had succeeded in blotting from her mind her awareness of herself as a woman and her capacity for love and desire—and had been helped in this by the memory of betrayal. Yet hate Grant Goodman and the type of man he had to be she might, but she couldn't quite erase from her mind the image of his knee so nearly brushing hers, the strength of his beautifully made body, his voice, his hands...

She licked her lips and opened her make-up drawer a little frantically as she thought, I don't believe this. I must need a holiday—for God's sake, Briony, you must be mad, and don't ever let him suspect! Just think of what he said...

It did the trick. Her hands stilled and her eyes grew cold and she said something extremely uncomplimentary to his unknown mother beneath her breath.

'I was imagining it,' she told her image with a sigh of relief, but there was the sudden light of battle in her eyes as she squared her shoulders. And she applied her make-up with a light, steady hand.

'What's he like?'

Linda Cross was manning the reception desk although they were in the office behind but could see the desk through a striped glass window. She was in her mid-twenties, bright and efficient but with a deeply romantic soul.

Briony put her mug of coffee down and pulled the latest fax from the machine. 'Who?'

Linda rolled her eyes. 'That gorgeous man who went on the walk with you, who else? Mr Grant Goodman.'

Briony read through the fax, registered the pleasing fact that they would be fully booked next week and murmured, 'So-so. Who is he?'

'So-so?' Linda looked affronted. 'Briony— don't tell me you didn't notice.'

Briony looked up. 'What?'

Linda sighed. 'How tall he is, not to mention wildly attractive, how experienced he looks and sort of autocratic.' She shivered with pleasure, then grimaced. 'And rather nice in an entirely uninterested way.'

'Nice,' Briony repeated with a twist of her lips. 'I wouldn't actually accuse him of being nice.'

Linda opened her eyes. 'He upset you?'

'Not exactly,' Briony lied, 'but we didn't— how should I put it?—entirely hit it off.'

'Briony—a guest is a guest is a guest——'

'All right!' Briony held up her hand with a grin. 'Spare me my own lectures. Uh—do you have any idea who he is?'

'No—what do you mean? Is he Robert Redford's younger brother in disguise?'

'I meant,' Briony said drily, 'do we know who's paying for him, is it connected with business at all, have you, in your own inimitable way, discovered what he does for a living or anything like that?'

'He only arrived late yesterday afternoon, Briony,' Linda said wryly. 'Give me a chance! But he's paying for himself on a personal Mastercard of which I have an impression, his home address is Sydney, his booking was made by phone from Sydney, and no, I was unable to glean anything further,' she said regretfully. 'Other than that his luggage looked pretty classy and expensive but not new and he arrived from Launceston in a hire car.'

'Oh, well,' Briony said with a shrug, 'it doesn't matter. How's Lucien?'

'Our own Alpine guide and cheap charmer of women?' Linda said with unusual hauteur. 'He's got the worst cold you've ever seen, which is no less than he deserves.'

'I warned you about Lucien, Linda. All that Gallic charm is just a little too— blinding.'

'He certainly believes in spreading it around—don't be surprised if we have a flu epidemic on our hands,' Linda replied tartly. 'Unfortunately the guided Cradle Mountain hike is on tomorrow's activity list. I don't know if he'll be well enough to make it.'

Briony muttered beneath her breath. 'Can we cancel it?'

Linda grimaced. 'I've got four names for it already and they're all really keen—two couples, both honeymooners. And since you decided to take his place today I decided to check with you before doing any cancelling.

Briony closed her eyes. The climb to one of the twin peaks of Cradle Mountain was an eight-hour walk and definitely not a soft one but it was one she'd done often over the past year. Guiding a troop of people along it who were often less fit than they thought they were was not, though, she thought, how she felt like spending the next day. 'How long are they staying?' she asked.

'Leaving the day after.'

Briony grimaced. 'Damn. All right, we'll let it stand and hope for fog and rain. What else?' She leafed through a sheaf of faxes.

'Nothing much—other than reservations. I relayed your disapproval of the last lot of lobsters and threatened to go elsewhere. Oh— one washing machine refuses to work. I asked John ——' John was the gardener-cum-handyman '—to have a look at it but he was unable to fix it and the repair man can't get here until the day after tomorrow.' Linda grimaced. 'We do have a fair stock-pile of clean linen, though. And I was today in the happy position of being able to recommend either Cradle Mountain Lodge or Lemonthyme Lodge to people seeking reservations for next week.'

Briony smiled absently. Both Cradle Mountain and Lemonthyme had excellent reputations in the area but Linda was intensely ambitious for Heath House. And to be able to go from accepting the overflow from the other two, to doing a little overflowing herself, was obviously a source of great satisfaction. 'Keep up the good work,' she said with a warmer smile, then frowned. 'I wonder when our new owners are going to descend on us?'

'They don't actually take over for a couple of weeks, though, do they?'

'No.' Briony paused and thought of the kindly couple who had developed Heath House, a lifetime dream of theirs, and then been forced to place it on the market because of ill health. In fact, almost throughout its entire working existence input from the owners had been fragmented on that account and she couldn't help wondering how she would feel under closer supervision after such freedom—always assuming she was kept on... She also was extremely curious to know who had bought it, but on that subject her kindly bosses had been somewhat in the dark, apparently...

'I can only tell you the name of the company, which means nothing to me,' Frank Carter had told her on his last visit. 'It's certainly not one of the large tourist resort operators such as an airline or shipping company. Nor is it a hotel or motel chain—it's a bit of a mystery. We've only dealt, and at one remove via a real-estate agent, with their solicitors, who did assure us that they wanted to continue the operation as we had started it, that they'd been impressed with all they'd seen et cetera, et cetera. Briony,' he'd added sadly, 'so much of that is due to you, we'll never know how to thank you, and it's nearly breaking our hearts to have to part with the place. But after my last heart flutter...' He grimaced.

And she thought of the inspection party that had stayed for three days and gone into every aspect of the running of Heath House before they'd made an offer of purchase, and been politely unforthcoming. But they must have been impressed, she reassured herself not for the first time, and wasn't entirely reassured. Her years in the trade had seen quite a few new brooms and broken hearts.

'Where would you like to sit for dinner?' Linda enquired.

'As far away from Grant Goodman as possible,' Briony replied coldly before she could stop herself, then changed her mind. 'No, put me with him and the Weinbergs. I might as well get it over and done with.'

'Mmm!' Dora Weinberg said appreciatively. 'That trout was superb, Briony! So what do you do for a living, Grant?' she asked with superb candour.

'I have a cattle station in Queensland,' Grant Goodman returned with an engaging smile. 'That's on the mainland——'

And where your spirited, mettlesome mare once resided, no doubt, Briony thought bitterly, as Dora was delighted to be able to tell him they'd been to Queensland and describe exactly where.

In fact that took care of the conversation throughout dessert, a lovely concoction of strawberries and blackberries flavoured with kirsch and smothered in cream. Dwight and Dora were exceedingly interested in cattle stations, it transpired, and even Briony had to acknowledge, although a little sourly, that Grant Goodman responded to their curiosity well. And he managed to make the dry outback of Western Queensland come alive for them so that their eyes shone with enthusiasm and they responded with descriptions of the huge ranches back home.

So, Briony thought as she stirred her coffee, our friend is a wealthy grazier on the loose. He must be if he lives in Sydney...

At that point Grant excused himself, saying he thought he might make an early night of it, and he said goodnight to the three of them with absolutely no trace of innuendo towards Briony—nor had there been, she realised, apart from the first comprehensive summing up of her in fresh clothes, all evening. Which had left her feeling as if the wind had been taken out of her sails... So what is he playing at? she wondered.

It was Dora who sat back with a little sigh, 'Such a *nice* man,' she said happily, and turned to Briony with a naughty twinkle in her eyes, 'and a bachelor by the sound of it, to boot. How old would you say he is? Late thirties?' She didn't wait for corroboration but nodded decisively. 'A good time for a man to settle down, I always think.'

'But I was twenty-one and you were nineteen when we settled down,' Dwight pointed out ruefully.

'And you always were an old softie, Dwight Weinberg,' his wife said cheerfully. 'So was I. But someone like Grant Goodman would be perfect for a mature girl like Briony, you mark my words!'

Unable to decide why the coupling of 'mature' and 'girl' should make her feel distinctly uncomfortable, on top of all the other things she felt, Briony was unusually vivacious as she supervised the nightly feeding of the possums, et cetera, from the west porch.

'Now that's a pademelon—I know it sounds like a fruit but it's a small sort of wallaby, as you can see. Oh, and look, there's a devil! They're not as common as the others so we're lucky tonight.' And she embarked on her spiel about feeding the native fauna only fruit and vegetables, otherwise they could develop 'lumpy jaw', a condition that could be fatal—and was rewarded as a couple of wombats lumbered up, causing her guests to go into further transports.

She was further rewarded by the fact that most people decided on an early night, a phenomenon that was directly attributable to the wonderful weather that had seen them all out hiking, and by ten o'clock the lounge was empty.

But as she made her last tour of duty, dimming lamps and plumping cushions, Grant Goodman came in.

'Ah,' he said, and stopped as his eyes fell on her. 'Am I too late, Briony?'

She straightened and eyed him warily. He wore the same charcoal trousers and pale grey shirt he'd worn to dinner but with a fine wool charcoal pullover added. 'Too late for what?'

He lifted an eyebrow. 'What did you have in mind?'

She tightened her mouth, which he observed then said mildly, 'A nightcap, as a matter of fact. I couldn't sleep—the stillness and silence is absolutely deafening.'

'Not at all,' she said, recovering smoothly. 'Would you like to take it to your chalet? It might be a bit lonely here, as you can see.'

'No, thank you. I'd much rather you joined me.'

'I'm sorry, but I have rather a full day tomorrow and I should go to bed.' She said it with just the friendly touch she was so adept at using and moved to behind the bar. 'What would you like?'

He sat down on a stool and studied her for a moment. 'Do you always do the things you should?'

'Always,' she said firmly and brightly and in top 'guest-dealing' mode. 'Don't you?'

'Not always, no,' he said thoughtfully, and their eyes locked although she couldn't say why those three words should have the power to arrest her gaze, but they did until she made herself look away and take down a glass.

'Scotch? Brandy? Or would you like a liqueur? We have an extensive range.'

'So I see. But I'll have a brandy and dry, thank you. Where do you hail from, Briony, as a matter of interest?'

She poured the brandy, splashed in the dry and slid it towards him, then reached for a bar card. 'Sydney too, but a highly uninteresting suburb and without the refreshing change of being able to hop off to your own cattle station when the mood took you.'

He smiled faintly. 'Cattle stations in the flesh can be dusty, unromantic, hard-working places.'

'Dear me, then you misled Dwight and Dora a bit, didn't you?'

He shrugged, looked amused and answered obliquely, 'Is this prejudice you're exhibiting directed towards cattle station owners and graziers in general or simply me?'

Briony showed her teeth rather than smiled and for the life of her couldn't help saying, 'A bit of both, probably.'

'So does that mean —— ' his long fingers played around the bottom of his glass '——you see graziers as a privileged class while you were not?'

Briony stared at him then said drily, 'What does it matter? I'm —— '

'Going to bed?' he supplied softly. 'You'd be much better joining me and getting it all off your chest. Cheers.' He raised his glass.

Briony contemplated stalking regally away, decided it would look more like an angry rout and quite out of keeping with her position, and reached for another glass. But all she poured into it was mineral water. 'Cheers,' she said brusquely.

'You don't drink?'

'I do drink alcohol sometimes,' she replied precisely. 'When I'm in a party mood.'

'I see. What shall we talk about now?'

She opened her mouth to ask him where he'd heard about her, something that had been lying heavily on her mind since their exchange in the bus, but closed it sharply and said instead, 'You choose, Mr Goodman, since you're so determined to have this conversation.'

He drank some of his brandy, put his glass down slowly and looked her over dispassionately. 'Tell me more about this disadvantaged growing-up you had.'

'I didn't say that!'

'It's what you led me to believe, however.'

She shrugged. 'My father died when I was ten and my mother had a bit of a battle to raise two children, but it wasn't an unhappy childhood.' She smiled mechanically.

'How did you get into this business?'

'When I was eighteen and doing a book-keeping course, I got a part-time job as a barmaid in a city hotel. In twelve months I was running that bar then I graduated to reception work and so on and so on.'

He narrowed his hazel eyes. 'You *must* have great flair with people and unusual organisational skills.'

'I do,' she agreed in an entirely deadpan way.

He smiled. 'Was this then a step up the ladder or down?'

'Oh, up,' she said sweetly and dared him, with her eyes, to challenge it. But it appeared that Grant Goodman, who if he knew one thing about her must know more, was not prepared to show his hand. In any other than a supremely sly way, she thought with contempt.

'And what,' he enquired lazily, 'is going on behind those beautiful blue eyes now?'

She grimaced. 'Nothing that's for public consumption.'

'You may rely on me to keep it all private,' he murmured with a significant glint in his hazel eyes as they roamed from her mouth to her breasts beneath the blue and silver dress.

'A private pillory—is that what you mean?' she shot back despite the faint flush that came to her cheeks. 'Then you're wasting your time, Mr Goodman. I don't care what you think about me or what you say to me.'

'Even although you could be tempted to—er—fancy me as I do you?'

She gasped and tried to cover it. 'That situation will never arise,' she said through her teeth.

He raised an amused eyebrow. 'It occurred to me that it already had. It occurred to me,' he said idly, 'that you were acting strangely towards me right from the start.'

'Now that,' Briony said, controlling her temper with difficulty, 'is the worst case of wishful thinking I've encountered for a long time. All I was reacting to was the growing knowledge that you're one of those unfortunate men who eyes any passable girl or woman.'

He laughed and said peacefully, 'I don't. I think the problem is you're so much more than just passable. You're quite gorgeous, in fact. You're...' he paused '...not without experience, apparently, but neither am I—I think we'd deal extremely well together. And there's another consideration to take into account from your point of view, of course— my much maligned cattle station has been quite good to me—which is to say, I wouldn't leave you to walk away from me empty-handed.'

Briony was possessed of a mad impulse to pick up her glass and hurl it at him but she restrained herself—just. She did, however, empty her untasted mineral water down the sink and say crisply, 'Your thought processes amaze me and fill me with disgust, if you would really like to know. And I am now going to bed whether you like it or not.'

'Well, I would obviously like it much more if we were to do that together but I can wait.' He drained his glass and stood up, observed her contorted expression with a curiously dry smile then said mildly, 'Goodnight, Briony. By the way, I put my name down for the Cradle Mountain hike tomorrow. I believe you're leading it so I thought you'd like to know.'

CHAPTER TWO

'I DON'T care if he's dying—I want to see Lucien, Linda!'

'All right, all right! But it is nearly eleven o'clock.'

Briony shrugged callously. 'And why didn't you tell me Grant Goodman had booked to go on the Cradle Mountain hike? And why did you tell *him* I was leading it?'

'Because he *asked*, because he didn't make the booking until after dinner just before I went off duty—which I still am,' Linda said plaintively. 'Anyway, what was I supposed to do? Tell him he couldn't? Tell *you* to break a leg——'

Briony held up a hand. 'Just get Lucien.'

'Briony, Briony,' Lucien said thickly a few minutes later, 'you think I play-act? You think this?' He looked at her injuredly.

Briony sighed. There was no mistaking his pallor and heavy eyes or the wheezy way he talked.

'You think you can't do it?' Lucien enquired. 'You can do it! You have the first-aid course, you have the knowledge of the mountain——'

'Of course I can do it,' Briony retorted. 'I just don't want to. Don't you think I have enough to do as it is?'

Lucien shrugged. 'Then cancel,' he suggested. 'Explain that I, Lucien du Plessis, guide extrordinaire, have been forced to my bed with a cold.'

'Go back to your bed, Lucien,' Briony said wearily. 'Perhaps it will snow.'

Of course it didn't. It was a perfect day and, according to the Cradle Mountain Visitor Information Centre, which had a weather fax, was likely to remain so.

To make matters worse, as she strode up to the laundry to inspect the errant washer, who should be out taking an early morning stroll but Grant Goodman?

'Good morning, Briony,' he said cheerfully and fell into step beside her.

'Good morning,' she replied briefly with one bare, swift glance at his tall figure.

'Or not such a good morning for you,' he said gently and ran one hand absently through his thick, tawny hair.

'What do you mean? Why shouldn't it be?'

'It crossed my mind that you might have spent the night praying for a blizzard.'

She bit her lip, coloured then said with bleak honesty, 'You're right. But never let it be said I can't cope with *you*, Mr Goodman; I've certainly had plenty of experience of men on the make.'

'So I'd heard,' he commented and, before she could respond, added, 'What, may I enquire, are you off to ''cope'' with at the moment? In such a flaming hurry and with such a militant look on your face,' he said softly.

Briony compressed her lips, nearly bit right through her bottom one, in fact, then said steadily, 'A washing machine on the blink, Mr Goodman, a washing machine, that's all. And you don't need to accompany me; in fact we prefer guests not to stray into the staff quarters where this machine is located.'

'Poor machine,' he murmured. 'Do your fabled managerial skills extend to mechanics or is this machine liable to receive a kick in the guts? I only ask that,' he said swiftly as she rounded on him but with pure, wicked laughter in his eyes, 'because I do know something about machines. Or are you embarrassed by your staff quarters? You have only to say.'

Briony breathed deeply. 'Not at all, Mr Goodman. Actually at Heath House we pride ourselves on the comfort of our staff quarters. And since you're—frothing at the mouth to inspect them, please be my guest.'

'Thank you,' he said equably. 'Had you noticed that we trade insults well, Briony?'

'I have noticed—— No,' she said icily, 'enough is enough, Mr Goodman. Here we are.' And she gave him a brief tour of the facilities and was somewhat soothed by the fact that everything was spick and span, as she always insisted, then she led him into the laundry where the startled laundry maid indicated the faulty machine. And Briony hoped against malicious hope that he would prove useless.

'Ah,' Grant Goodman said, 'I had one of these heavy duty commercial ones installed on—my cattle station. And we've found that things have a tendency to get stuck beneath the agitator, which comes apart so.' He worked for a few moments then pulled out the agitator, groped around and held up in his fingers a large blue button. 'I'd be very surprised if it didn't work now.'

It did and Briony could have *kicked* it. 'Thank you,' she said coldly as they left the laundry.

'My pleasure,' he returned. 'It's comforting to know there are still some instances when it's handy to have a man around the place.'

'I have a man around the place—several,' she retorted. 'Just none conversant with washing machines,' she added drily.

'Never mind,' he consoled.

'Who said I minded?' she said sharply and could have kicked herself. 'Mr Goodman —— ' she stopped in the middle of the path '——would you very much mind making your way back alone? Breakfast is imminent and I have some other things to do. Besides which I feel we have a long enough day ahead of us as it is.'

'Certainly,' he said promptly, 'although I fail to see how I could have offended you this time.'

Briony clenched her fists on another mad impulse, to slap his face this time—something that clever hazel gaze was immediately alert to.

'My dear Briony,' he drawled, his eyes travelling back to her face, 'you really shouldn't get so worked up this early in the day. It can't be good for your digestion. See you later.' And he turned away and strolled down the path with all the unhurried easy grace of a superbly fit male animal.

She was still breathing heavily as she checked the backpacks that Heath House hired out for hikes, but managed to get herself under better control as she drove the minibus to the Waldheim car park, and explained that the weather could be highly unpredictable around Cradle Mountain, which was why they had to carry warmer and waterproof clothes. Grant Goodman made no attempt to sit next to her this time and the two honeymoon couples looked fit enough but only one pair had any climbing experience.

She also explained, as she drove, about the track they'd be taking—the Overland Track via Crater Lake and Falls—and how it offered the easier ascent to Marions Lookout

rather than the Lake Dove side. And she duti-
fully signed them into the ranger's book at
the car park.

'Is that really necessary?' Wendy, one of
the inexperienced honeymooners, a petite
blonde, asked.

'Of course,' Don, her husband, said with
a trace of impatience. 'If you get lost, stolen
or strayed, they know to come looking for
you.'

'But we're not going to get any of those
things, Briony, are we?' Wendy said
nervously.

'I certainly hope not,' Briony replied brac-
ingly, then relented. 'Enjoy yourself; it's a
wonderful experience on a day like today.'

And it certainly was as she led them across
the button-grass plain below Waldheim's. The
air was crisp and clear, the sky blue and
cloudless and the colours of grass, rock, bush
and woodland wonderful. And once across
the plain they climbed steadily, with her in
front and Grant Goodman bringing up the
rear, past the musical, lush and cool depths
of Crater Falls and the deep blue glacial
depths of Crater Lake surrounded by two-
hundred metre stark cliffs sprinkled with de-

ciduous beech. It was as they reached a saddle in the hills above Crater Lake that she called the first halt.

'We're going well, troops, but let's take a bit of a breather. The next bit is one of the trickiest.' And she heaved her pack off and sat down. Grant Goodman sat down beside her, doing likewise.

She glanced at him briefly then opened her water bottle and took a sip.

'Lovely spot, Briony,' he murmured, again doing likewise.

'Yes.'

'Would I get my face slapped if I suggested that your pack is heavier than mine and offered an exchange?'

It was true. In her capacity as guide, she had a first-aid kit and a mobile phone in her pack, but she glanced at him again, with scorn, and said quietly, 'I think I'll reserve my face-slapping for your—more unpleasant suggestions. Thank you for the offer but I'll be fine.'

'As you wish,' he said evenly. He wore khaki shorts, proper boots and, like her, orange spats over his socks as protection against snakes, and by an unusual coincidence they both wore bright yellow T-shirts. 'Young Wendy,' he added, more naturally, 'is going to slow us down.'

'Don't I know it,' Briony said without thinking. 'She's puffed already. I'm almost tempted to suggest they go back; it's simple enough from here. But I've got the feeling she's not about to admit anything.'

'Go ahead,' he remarked. 'I'd be interested to see how you handle it.'

'And I'd be interested to see how *you* would handle it,' she retorted.

He smiled but there was a mocking little glint in his hazel eyes. 'I'm not being paid to handle anything at the moment but we could use a relay system with her pack up the steeper bits. That would make it easier for her.'

Briony raised an eyebrow. 'Your concern is touching, Mr Goodman. Don't tell me your roving eye has so soon been diverted from me to a girl barely twenty who is on her *honeymoon*, moreover?' She stood up lithely.

He followed suit in one swift easy movement. 'Being bitchy doesn't become you, Briony,' he murmured. 'And any concern I feel is for a poor kid who's probably been coerced into this by her new husband against her better judgement and who would rather die than let him down.'

Briony flushed, opened her mouth then turned away without speaking. But then she squared her shoulders and dipped her head in silent acknowledgement, a gesture she didn't know whether he appreciated as an admission of guilt, and walked over to Wendy and Don.

'Wendy, you and I are going to tackle Marions together. It's not that easy for a novice so I'll be able to give you some tips.' And she smiled warmly at the other girl. 'Don can follow right behind.'

By the time they reached Marions Lookout, she felt as if she'd virtually carried Wendy the whole way; she'd certainly guided her up step by steep, difficult step, all the time encouraging her and making light not only of the girl's lack of stamina but lack of sure-footedness, as it turned out.

But she was rewarded with a glowing smile as Wendy collapsed in a heap and gasped out her thanks.

'You're welcome,' she said wryly. 'We'll make a climber of you, you'll see.' But she glanced at Cradle Mountain ruefully and slumped down herself, avoiding both Grant

Goodman's and Don's eyes. Don had tended to be irritated with his wife, causing Briony to think that if things were like this on their honeymoon the rest of their life could be hell, but Grant Goodman, she had to admit although she hated it, had been unobtrusively helpful and had carried Wendy's pack up the last bit himself.

The rest of that hike she was to remember for a long time. From Marions Lookout towards Cradle Mountain the path was fairly easy for a time and the views breathtaking. And the vegetation was distinctly Alpine— crunchy moss and lichens peppered with tiny flowers and pools of water everywhere and contrasting with the dust and granite rubble of the path.

But it wasn't the scenery that day that stayed in her memory, it was the task of getting young Wendy up the steep, final assault to the summit, and then getting her down again and doing it all with the appearance of enjoyment. It was the memory of her husband Don grumbling at her and then at everyone, including those who advertised this hike as within the reach of experienced *walkers*. 'You need to be a bloody fly on the wall,' he'd said, and lapsed into angry silence when Briony had reminded him that everyone who booked on the Cradle Mountain Hike was told of its rigours. It was the memory, on the way down—with Grant Goodman quietly and expertly getting Wendy down Marions this time—of trying to rescue the day for the other couple and somehow succeeding, and even getting them all back to Heath House full of the spirit of adventure and achievement— Which just goes to show what short memories *some* people have, she'd thought drily.

It was the memory of finally closing herself into her suite, exhausted and drained, then clenching her teeth when someone knocked, and it turned out not to be Linda as she'd expected at her sitting-room door but Grant Goodman with a bottle of champagne and two glasses.

'How the hell did you get in?' she blazed as she stepped backwards.

He raised a bland eyebrow. 'I bribed your receptionist. I came to say bravo! I've rarely before seen such a truly gritty performance.' He closed the door and looked around. He'd already showered and changed into jeans and a sweater, it had cooled down perceptibly at last although Briony found herself feeling anything but cool.

Dusty and dishevelled, her clothes stiff where they had been sweat-soaked, her muscles aching, she closed her eyes, rubbed her brow briefly and said, 'Would you believe me if I told you that it's nothing personal but the last thing I feel like doing now is drinking champagne with you? I —— '

'No,' he said with a faint grin, and set the glasses down. 'I mean to say I'm sure it is personal, knowing you, dear Briony, but if you would have me believe you're also dying to have a shower, that I can understand. I'll wait,' he added, popping the champagne cork with the minimum of fuss and starting to pour.

Briony stared at him helplessly and wondered a little wildly how she could have him thrown out.

'Take yours with you,' he added gravely, handing her a brimming, bubbling glass.

'You're—unbelievable.' She stared at the glass then into his hazel eyes. 'You can't just do this.'

'Do what?' he queried, picking up her hand and closing it around the glass. 'Is there something so wrong in it? You chivvied that kid up and down a mountain today and I carried her pack while her not-so-bright husband complained nearly all the time. Why shouldn't we share a drink? I think we deserve it.'

Briony opened her mouth then closed it because she knew that without Grant Goodman's discreet back-up today it would have been an absolute fiasco. And in other circumstances she would have been grateful and impressed... Her shoulders sagged suddenly. 'I really don't understand you,' she said bitterly, 'and I'm going to have a shower whether you like it or not. I must warn you I *don't* expect it to alter my frame of mind, which is to say that while I am grateful for your help today I resent this intrusion, but short of calling on the chef, who is our behind-the-scenes bouncer, and creating an unpleasant scene, I can't think what else to do with you!'

'So put that in your pipe and smoke it, Mr Goodman,' he said softly, his eyes glinting with devilry. 'Well said, Briony! The syntax was a trifle convoluted but the sentiment obviously heartfelt. Go on,' he said kindly. 'I'll still be here.'

Briony leant back against her bedroom door, which she had just closed less than gently on her uninvited guest, realised she was clutching a glass of champagne, half of which she'd spilt, and took a gulp of the rest of it. I should have had him thrown out, she raged inwardly. I will! As soon as I've cleaned myself up.

She was still raging inwardly as she took a shower rather than the spa bath she would have loved and donned a misty blue tracksuit. She'd washed her hair and she merely ran her fingers through it as it started to curl riotously and she rubbed moisturiser into her face, but, apart from smoothing her eyebrows with her fingers, added no make-up, not even lipstick to her mutinously set mouth. I'm going to have it out with this man once and for all, she thought. Guest or no guest, I will not put up with this!

She was back in about fifteen minutes and was further incensed to see him sitting quietly on her settee with his long legs stretched out, staring into the fire he'd started in her log stove. Not that she wouldn't have done the same—Cradle Mountain had finally lived up to its reputation for unpredictable weather and it was now raining.

'Do make yourself at home,' she said sardonically, 'but I wouldn't get too comfortable if —— '

He looked up and raised a wry eyebrow at her. 'You've decided to call up the bouncer?'

She bit her lip but soldiered on. 'No, not this time, but dinner starts in about ten minutes and I'm sure we can say all that needs to be said in that time.'

'Oh?' He looked amused. 'Such as?'

'Such as why you're so sure you can play these games with me, Mr Goodman,' she said crisply. 'You hinted yesterday that you knew something about me. I can only assume you feel it gives you some sort of hold over me. Well, I'm prepared to call your bluff. My last job was with a Sydney hotel owned by a family of hoteliers who now specialise in "boutique" hotels and —— '

'The Semple family.'

'Yes—do you know them?'

'I'm sure most people in the trade have heard of the Semples,' he said idly.

Briony frowned but continued doggedly. 'Well, I left it because I was perceived by some members of that family as trying to break up the son and heir's marriage——'

'Did you?' he interjected quietly.

Briony gritted her teeth. 'That,' she said grimly, 'concerns only three people——'

'That may be,' he broke in again, 'but enough other people were apparently in the know for you to have acquired—something of a reputation.'

'Indeed,' she agreed icily. 'A reputation as a scarlet woman, a seductress, a gold-digger and a lot of other things I probably don't even know about.' She smiled coldly. 'Things that you have latched on to obviously, and I really can't tell you how much I despise you for it. But, be that as it may, I've already paid for any mistakes I may have made. So, what I'm trying to impress on you, Mr Goodman, is that you're wasting your time. You can neither blackmail me nor cajole me into— anything.'

'Do your employers know why you left Sydney?'

'As a matter of fact, when I tried to tell them, they said that what was past history should remain so and it was my qualifications they were more interested in. Now I'm sure you might think they're a very naïve, trusting couple but I've done absolutely nothing to betray that trust, believe me. As for my future employers——' she said baldly, then paused and shrugged. 'I haven't met them yet—you probably know that the place has been sold? Of course,' she said as he nodded. 'Well, if it's them you're going to hold over my head, assuming you can find them, you're welcome to carry the tale of my misdeeds to them, but I'd be surprised if they haven't gone into my background quite thoroughly already. And if they're going to place more emphasis on my... love life than my managerial skills, so be it. I'm certainly not going to spend the rest of my life trying to hide it, or kowtowing to people with sick minds like yourself.'

'So you don't think it's of any concern to your future employers?'

'*What*?'

'Well,' he said easily, 'that their guests might be subject to a—how shall I put it?— designing woman.'

'That is so far from the truth, as you yourself could prove to them, Mr Goodman,' she said with contempt, 'were you anything but a —— '

'Slimy reptile?' His eyes glinted.

'I was planning to be even more inventive,' she said grimly. 'I'll forgo the pleasure. Ah, there goes the dinner gong. Please don't let me keep you any longer.'

He stood up and quite brazenly walked over to her phone. 'I have a better idea. Let's get our dinner sent in here.'

'No... *Look*... this is too much,' Briony stammered. 'Don't you dare use that phone!'

He did. He picked it up and said into it, 'Linda? Grant Goodman. Would you present my compliments to the chef and ask him to deliver two dinners to Briony's suite? We have a lot of business to discuss. Thank you.'

Briony stared at him, her mouth open, her eyes arrested and all sorts of blinkers falling off and a sudden sinking feeling at the pit of her stomach. 'Are you ... are you who I think you are?' she spat, ignoring what her stomach was doing, so great was her rage. 'Are you the new owner?'

His lips twisted. 'None other,' he agreed mildly.

'*Oh* ... I could kill you —— '

'You've already tried that once.'

It was too much. Briony launched herself at him, her eyes flashing blue fire, and a string of some unladylike invective issuing from her lips. '*You* ...'

But he fielded her attack with little effort and as he clamped her wrists together in an iron grip he even had the gall to laugh a little, then said, 'My dear Briony, you're absolutely splendid in a rage but don't you think this is a little undignified?'

'Undignified!' she spat at him. 'I have light-years to travel in the undignified stakes compared to you! Passing yourself off as a guest, making all sorts of unspeakable passes at me—things that crawl out of holes have more dignity than you!'

'And you've already told me *that* too——'

'Well, I'm telling you again. And I'll be doing it again and again,' she flashed, 'you miserable *skunk*!'

'Now that,' he mused, 'is a little uncalled for, I feel, and worthy of retaliation.' He gazed meditatively down at her heaving breasts, her triumphant, angry eyes, and released her wrists and pulled her into his arms. 'I wouldn't scream, kick or bite,' he murmured, 'because that might prompt me to put you over my knee—— No, I really think if you dish it out the way you do, you should be prepared to take the consequences.'

Briony only had a moment to realise what the consequences were to be but it was long enough to gather herself to do everything he had warned her against except scream—and discover it was quite useless. He *was* as strong as a lion and it was like dashing herself uselessly against a brick wall.

'No,' she whispered at last on a sobbing little breath, 'I don't want to be kissed and only a bastard would make me...'

'I wonder?' he said drily. 'But why wonder? We'll never know until we try it and I think it would be fair to say the thought of it has been lying between us since we set eyes on each other—haven't *you* wondered whether your extreme aversion to me isn't based on a sense of curiosity you despise yourself for?'

'Your ego,' she whispered, 'is monumental.'

'Maybe; we'll see.' And he lowered his mouth to hers. She went rigid within the prison of his arms, expecting a brutal invasion of her mouth, but it didn't come. When she kept her lips tight shut, she felt him smile against her skin and his lips wandered to her cheekbone, to her eyelids, also clamped tightly shut, and he said barely audibly, 'Your hair smells wonderful. Have you thought how well-matched we are? I must admit it crossed my mind today while I watched you striding up that mountain.' And his wandering lips moved at will over her smooth skin. 'Don't talk if you don't want to,' he added gravely. 'I too have the feeling the less said the better.'

'So you jolly well should...' She couldn't help herself although it was only a thread of sound.

'Well, I actually meant —— ' he moved one hand up and caressed the nape of her neck and the fine skin behind her ears '—that what we do to each other could have more impact than mere words—as your breathing seems to indicate right now, Briony.'

It was true, unfortunately. From breathing raggedly through sheer physical exertion, she was now breathing raggedly because of another kind of exertion—that of trying to remain passive beneath this unexpectedly gentle assault on her senses. I don't believe it, she thought, and made one final effort.

'I gather you're determined to kiss me, Goodman,' she said tightly. 'You've certainly overpowered me and are making those sorts of overtures. Now I must warn you I don't believe in lying back and thinking of England, I certainly don't believe any retaliation is due, your methods,' she said scathingly, 'had to be about as low as any one could go! But unfortunately there's a limit to my strength, so why don't you get it over and done with?'

He laughed softly. 'That's my Briony, but I don't get a kick out of kissing women against their will.'

'You could have fooled me!'

'No, although I might have experienced the base desire to test you out a bit,' he said with a glint of humour, 'but I do think you might be fooling yourself. Think of it this way. How—rewarding would it have been for us to have done that walk on our own today? Don't you think it would have given you a lot of pleasure to have matched me stride for stride? To have had company to appreciate the wonders of Cradle Mountain without worrying about a lot of novices, someone to talk to, to sit next to and drink in the view. Someone, moreover,' he said very quietly, and cupped her cheek, 'who you knew would bring you home and take you to bed to—celebrate a wonderful day.'

Briony's lips parted and she stared with a mixture of bemusement and horror into his eyes as she wondered how he could be so diabolically clever. How he could unearth a corner of her soul she'd tried so resolutely to bury this past year—how he could hold up her loneliness to her and at the same time match their physical compatability to it unerringly.

His eyes narrowed briefly at the shock in hers then his mouth closed over hers. She shuddered slightly and he held her closer so that not only could she taste him as his tongue probed hers but feel his body on hers, and feel the tips of her breasts swell at the contact with the hard wall of his chest; feel his hands move down her back to the flare of her hips through her tracksuit trousers, then, shockingly slip beneath the elasticised waist so that he was caressing her skin and sliding his fingers beneath the flimsy silk of her panties.

She tried to break away then. 'No...'

'No? All right,' he murmured obligingly, lifting his head, his eyes curiously heavy-lidded. 'I'm open to suggestion.' And he slid his hands beneath her top and cradled her back instead.

She made a husky, desperate little sound which he stifled by starting to kiss her again, but lightly on the lips this time, then turning his attention to her throat. She swayed in his arms but his will, his expertise were too much for her. She was invaded by a sweet, spreading, trembling warmth; she found she felt both safe and on the edge of something wild and dangerous, something primitive yet oddly fitting between two people who were also enemies . . .

She found, when his mouth returned to hers, that she could kiss him back helplessly as pang after pang of desire rippled through her like liquid fire.

The knock on the door was what brought her tumbling back to earth. 'Oh,' she whispered, tearing her lips away. 'Oh, God— *dinner*!'

'Dinner,' he agreed wryly but took his time releasing her. Then he straightened her top, brushed her lips with one finger and said, staring directly down into her eyes, 'If that was thinking of England, Briony, then lucky England, but I'm tempted to think you're starved of something, and it's not dinner.'

CHAPTER THREE

IT WAS like a dash of cold water in the face.

Briony stepped back and closed her eyes on a sudden, ridiculous spurt of angry tears while Grant Goodman answered the knock.

It was the chef pushing a laden trolley, his round face wreathed in smiles, followed by Linda, who looked nervous.

'Dinner for two, sir!' Chef said, and rubbed his hands. 'How do you do?' he added. 'I'm Peter Marsden and Linda tells me you're our new owner.'

Linda bit her lip. 'Briony,' she said anxiously, 'I didn't know what to do. I didn't *know* until he told me a short while ago...just before he came in here.'

'It's quite all right, Linda,' Briony said coolly. 'Mr Goodman's ways are a little strange, that's all.'

Chef Marsden's eyebrows all but disappeared beneath his tall cap and Linda swallowed visibly, but Grant Goodman took control with a faint wry smile.

'I'm sure we'll all find things a little strange until we get used to each other,' he said smoothly. 'But so far I'm quite impressed and it would probably help if we all relaxed and just got on with the job.'

Chef Marsden accepted this with alacrity. 'My sentiments entirely! May I present your dinner, sir?' he added and, with a flourish, removed some silver covers. 'Home-made mushroom soup, roast beef, fresh garden beans, sautéd carrots and roast potatoes with a gravy delicately flavoured with wine, and apple pie and cream. And I took the liberty of bringing along the Moorilla Pinot Noir '89, which, besides being a local wine, has an excellent reputation. *Bon appetit*!' he said jovially, and started to withdraw, motioning Linda to do the same. But Linda was staring at Briony's wooden expression and proved recalcitrant.

'It's quite all right, Linda,' Grant Goodman said patiently. 'She'll be perfectly safe with me.'

Briony looked ceilingwards with gritted teeth and turned away. Linda left in some confusion.

'You . . .'

'Here...' They spoke together and Briony turned to discover that he was offering a glass of champagne. 'We might as well finish it. Take it, Briony,' he said drily, and when she did, although mutinously, he turned back to the trolley and replaced the covers. 'Why don't you sit down?' he added over his shoulder. 'I really think we should unwind a bit before we attempt this feast.'

'I would be in no need of unwinding if it weren't for you,' she said quietly, but sat down suddenly.

'Because I kissed you? And you kissed me back?' He lifted a slightly mocking eyebrow at her and came to sit opposite.

'Because——' she swallowed and took refuge in a sip of her champagne '——you misled me, made a fool of me, told me lies about cattle stations——'

'That wasn't a lie. As a matter of fact I have two.'

'Lucky you!' Her eyes flashed. 'But you gave me to understand it was what you did for a living and——'

'It is what I do for a living, among other things.'

'So I gather,' she said contemptuously. 'How long have you been in hotels?'

'One way or another, quite a time. Look...' he said evenly.

'No! Why should I look at anything *you* want me to look at?' Her lips trembled but her eyes were dry. 'Nothing alters the fact that you propositioned me, *tested* me in a totally despicable way and...' She stopped and put a hand to her mouth, then drained her champagne.

He shrugged and laid his broad shoulders back. 'I've made a considerable investment in Heath House. I reserve the right to protect that investment as I see fit. But in point of fact I kissed you because I wanted to, not for any other reason. I also said what I did about a fitting way to end a day—and perhaps it's even more needed after a day like today— because I would like to do that too. So would you if you allowed yourself to be honest with yourself, Briony,' he said dispassionately.

'And how would you see me then?' she said with husky incredulity, her eyes dark and disbelieving. 'Not as a designing woman? Come now, Mr Goodman, I'm confused!'

His lips twisted. 'I don't think it's so con-
fusing at all. It happens all the time between
men and women. What they do about it is
another matter, and that's something we'll
have to decide. There's about a glass each left
in the bottle. Think you can handle it?'

'It doesn't happen all the time between men
and women,' she said through clenched teeth,
and barely noticed as he reached over and
filled her glass. 'Not the awful way you did
it, like some sort of blackmail!'

'Blackmail?' he said slowly, his eyes narrowed and unusually acute, then he shrugged.
'Have you never resorted to a little blackmail,
Briony?' He waited a moment as her eyes
widened and some colour started to steal up
her throat. He smiled drily. 'I'll tell you what
my intentions were,' he said easily, though.
'Yes, I had heard why you'd left Sydney, and
yes, if I'd perceived that you were truly a designing woman who imposed on guests, I
would have fired you ——'

'After you'd persuaded me to sleep with
you or before?' she said scathingly.

He looked amused. 'It was going to be
before you persuaded *me* to sleep with *you*,'

he said wryly. 'But the issue became a little unclear when I ... saw you.'

Briony breathed heavily. 'If I may say so, I think it's become abundantly clear—to me if not to you. And I think it's even clearer now; I really think it's going to be a case of sleep with me, Briony, or you lose your job!'

'Well, now,' he said idly, his eyes on her mouth, 'I must confess your attitude has awoken within me a certain—point of pride, perhaps. Which is to say that your very admirable in one sense but quite surprisingly pious air of superiority in another has made me rather determined to sleep with you because you can't help yourself. But I do also pride myself on being a sporting sort of bloke—well, sometimes,' he smiled crookedly, 'so your job is not in jeopardy, Briony, whatever the outcome of this—little war. What could be fairer than that?' He stood up and added matter-of-factly, 'Let's eat. And then I'd like to show you some of the plans I have for Heath House.'

'A heated indoor swimming-pool and sauna, a billiard-room, a squash court and a beauty shop,' Briony said distractedly. 'You'd never make them pay.'

'Not as things stand, no,' Grand Goodman agreed. 'But I also plan to put in the six more chalets originally planned for, although much more luxurious than originally planned, and to up the rates.'

Briony blinked at him. She'd tried to eat her dinner but had left most of it, and she'd refused the Moorilla. He'd shrugged and returned the bottle unopened to the trolley. He'd also not commented on her lack of appetite.

'You'd have to up the service, then,' she said, trying desperately to concentrate.

'Well, just providing these things would certainly be upgrading the facilities. You see, I have this sort of vision for Heath House. Most people who come here come to see Cradle Mountain and that will never change—it's a priceless drawcard. But what I have in mind is to create a drawcard almost as fascinating—a place people will want to come *back* to for itself, a place people will look forward to coming to even in the depths of winter, to pamper themselves in a heated pool, to have things to occupy them when the weather is shocking, to be able to have an energetic game of squash then the luxury of a massage, to be able to sip mulled wine around the pool while it snows outside, perhaps be able to play croquet on a synthetic surface—that kind of thing.'

'A resort that stands on its own in other words.'

'Precisely. A resort known throughout the mainland and hopefully further afield. Of course, to achieve that we *would* have to upgrade the service. We'd have to provide room service for a start and install more luxurious fittings and exquisite taste in the existing chalets. We'd have to be able to provide individual fax machines and direct international dialling for those who wanted it, et cetera, et cetera.'

'And you have the—wherewithal to achieve all this?'

He smiled absently. 'I have plenty of wherewithal, Briony.'

'Cattle must be even better than I thought,' she murmured and stared into the fire.

'Cattle, like all else, go through the good times and the bad,' he replied. 'But I've never been a believer in having all my eggs in the same basket. What do you think?'

Despite herself she couldn't help the little pulse of excitement she felt. It must be in my blood, she thought, this business, and to be in charge of a place of international renown, well, that's got to be the ultimate, hasn't it? But how can I possibly work with Grant Goodman—even assuming my job isn't in jeopardy over the issue of whether I sleep with him or not? She closed her eyes briefly and wondered if she was imagining it all.

'Briony?'

She stood up and went to pour the coffee Chef Marsden had so thoughtfully provided in an insulated silver flask. 'I think it would be important also to preserve some of the warmth and friendly spirit of the place as it is,' she said thoughtfully. 'I shouldn't like to see it become somewhere that the frightfully rich come to and don't—join in with each other at all. And no, that's not to do with any personal prejudice, as I can see from your quizzical expression you imagine I'm suffering from. It's to do with sheer common sense, I think. People tend to want to socialise after battling the elements or conquering

Cradle Mountain; that's what Dwight and Dora, for example, love about it.'

'I agree with you entirely,' he responded. 'And when done with the light hand you use it's invaluable. I'm sure Dwight and Dora will go home and remember the night before last when you all sang around the pianola almost as fondly as they'll remember Cradle Mountain.'

Briony glanced at him through her lashes then prosaically handed him a cup of coffee. 'There is one problem,' she said evenly, not sitting down herself because she felt too agitated to put it mildly.

'Let me guess—my ambitions concerning you?' he murmured.

'*Yes.*'

'I don't see that as a problem. The better we get along, the better for all concerned.'

'No, it's *not*,' she said forcefully. 'Assuming it were ever to be—purely hypothetically, of course——'

'Of course.'

'It would be a recipe for disaster, Mr Goodman. You can't seriously believe that to have me as your Tasmanian mistress—— ' her eyes flashed blue fire '——content to share your bed when you're here, and work away like a beaver when you're not, could ever work! That is what you're proposing, I assume?'

'I don't see why it shouldn't work,' he drawled. 'Not forever, naturally—although who knows?—but certainly long enough for us to achieve a lot for Heath House. It would take care of the lack of a man in your life without imposing any restraints on your career. Indeed, I think it would help you over this sticky patch, this self-imposed exile you're going through, quite nicely. How it would help me I probably don't have to go into graphic detail about. And ___ ' he stirred his coffee '—it would have the nice, sane and sensible aura of two people being level-headed about an issue that is remarkably prone to being clouded with a lot of often—useless emotion.' He looked up and his eyes were quite green in the firelight, and shockingly cynical.

Briony swallowed jerkily. 'Why are you— like this?' she whispered before she could stop herself.

His lips twisted. 'Why am I a realist, Briony? Is that what you're asking?'

'No! I mean—there has to be some reason . . . I couldn't have brought all this on myself, could I? Because . . . because of what happened in Sydney?' And for just a bare instant her eyes were pleading until she dropped her lashes sharply and with an indrawn breath of disbelief that she should lower herself to plead about anything to this man.

'What exactly did happen in Sydney?' he said after a moment.

'I told you,' she returned tautly.

'The only thing you actually told me, and I mean the only thing *you* admitted, was that any mistakes you'd made you'd paid for.'

'I should have thought that was patently obvious,' she said sardonically.

'Maybe, but it doesn't tell me whether you deliberately set out to break up a marriage to further your career in the ultimate way, or whether you fell wildly in love with the guy and just couldn't help yourself. I must say that your earlier . . . display when you were kissing me against your will——' he smiled slightly '—gave every indication of a very passionate nature.'

Briony went white but Grant Goodman continued unperturbed. 'Now if it was the second, well, we all do make mistakes. I myself,' he said placidly, 'married a girl who had the beauty and purity of looks one associates with all sorts of angelic virtues, only to discover that she had very cleverly disguised the fact that she had the soul of a tramp. Now that proved to be an extremely expensive mistake, I must tell you, Briony. It's just as well cattle were good then. So, what was it?'

'It was the first,' Briony said, contriving to mask her temper although her eyes glittered oddly, and only dimly aware of what he'd said about his marriage. But even as that sank in she said first with furious incredulity, 'Cattle!' Then, 'So that's why! And no doubt every woman since has been a scapegoat for your beautiful, faithless wife! Oh!'

He looked amused then reflective. 'A scapegoat? No, I don't think I'm as Freudian as that, but yes, one doesn't like to think one was as gullible as one once was, obviously, but one would be a fool not to know there are good women and ones that aren't so...angelic, and not necessarily because they're purely evil. One would also appreciate that your critical powers mature somewhat, so the mistakes you make when you were in your twenties are not the ones you're going to make later in life, hopefully.'

He looked at her wryly. 'How does that sum up? I freely admit I am a little—battle-scarred, Briony. As you are. Because, despite your protestation to the contrary, I don't think you can be entirely a gold-digger at heart, however it may have started out; you wouldn't have buried yourself here if you were. Which is why I have this strong feeling we would deal extremely well together. We've both had our illusions knocked about a bit, yet we are both red-blooded people, and you, my dear,' he said simply, 'are made for love.'

'Why...' her voice shook '...why don't you just say sex? Why bother to pretty it up at all?'

He shrugged. 'Sometimes the facts of life aren't pretty, are they? But between two people who genuinely desire each other I think it can be a bit more than just sex, don't you?' He waited and watched her mouth work but no sound came. 'There can be respect,' he went on, 'enjoyment, humour, there can be both giving and taking. And there can be the acknowledgement that, without some sort of release, you will be going around punching washing machines soon, Briony.'

She closed her eyes and said bitterly, 'Have you no other comforting words of wisdom for me?'

He raised an eyebrow at her tone. 'Such as?'

'Such as what *you* might do to release this frustration we're supposed to share. Or am I the only frustrated one around?'

He laughed. 'By no means. Who knows?'

'But not my job.' She opened her eyes and looked at him levelly. 'I mean—you won't go back on your word about my job, however frustrated you might feel?'

'I give you my word. As a matter of fact, we can talk about that if you like. Terms and salaries et cetera.'

She blinked. 'They're to change?'

'Naturally,' he said drily. 'You'll be in charge of a bigger operation, you'll be the one who'll have to smooth the path through a period of building operations—as it is, considering how you buck in and turn your hand to just about everything, I think you're rather underpaid. But my terms would be on a yearly contract basis.' He named an annual figure that caused Briony's eyes to widen. 'That impresses you?' he murmured, his eyes reading her expression accurately.

'It does,' she said slowly. 'But are you sure we haven't gone from blackmail to—bribery?'

'Not at all.' He looked unperturbed. 'You must be a little out of touch with the going rates, Briony,' he added with irony.

'I would rather—assuming I accepted,' she said a bit dazedly, 'work on a monthly basis.'

'I'm sure you would,' he said dispassionately. 'So you could up and off if our little war got out of hand. But I need someone to put at least a year's commitment into the place. Take it or leave it.'

A glint of anger entered her eyes. 'You can't expect me to make a decision like that in a matter of moments!' she protested.

'I'm not. You can think about it until I go back to Sydney if you like.' He shrugged. 'I'm merely letting you know that my terms, in *that* area——' he glanced at her significantly '—are not negotiable. And by the way, will you set up a staff meeting for me tomorrow morning? Ten o'clock would suit me best.'

'You don't actually own this place yet, Mr Goodman,' she was prompted for some foolish reason to say coldly.

He lay back and stared up at her. 'Oh, yes, I do, Briony,' he said softly. 'Lock, stock and barrel.'

'But...but,' she stammered, 'I thought settlement wasn't for another couple of weeks!'

'It wasn't supposed to be, but Frank Carter suffered another heart attack and is to undergo triple bypass surgery tomorrow. It was thought by all concerned to be—wise if it were brought forward. Settlement actually took place about the time I came in here this afternoon.'

'They didn't let me know?' she whispered, shock and hurt showing in her eyes.

He looked away briefly. 'That wasn't my doing,' he said evenly, however. 'I suppose the big question on their minds is, Will he survive?'

She sat down at last and put her hands to her face. 'I can't help wondering if this isn't all some—nightmare,' she said, more to herself than him.

He said nothing and after a little while she lifted her head to find him watching her idly. 'May I make a suggestion? he said eventually after their eyes had locked and she'd been unable to force herself to look away.

'No,' she said hoarsely. 'Not the kind I'm sure you have in mind.'

'Well,' he mused, 'I don't think it would be fair to expect you to sleep with me tonight, if that's what you thought I had in mind.' His lips quirked. 'Women can be strange creatures. Some of them appear to have no accepted sense of conscience at all, others get guilt complexes at the drop of a hat and I would hope we could clear the decks of all that before—we do the deed. But you could come here and accept some not precisely platonic but not *all-the-way* comfort.'

A few spurious tears sparkled on her lashes, mainly, she told herself, because she couldn't remember feeling more tired and less able to cope. She dashed them away fiercely, got up and poured herself a cup of black coffee. He watched her every movement but nothing changed about the relaxed way he was sitting, one arm slung across the back of her settee, his legs spread out before him. And nothing changed the fact that he looked big, entirely at home and like a lazy jungle cat toying with its prey.

She drank some coffee and then said crisply, 'Let's get this straight. Thank you for your offer to make me your mistress but I decline. Thank you also for the flattering offer you've made terms-and-salary-wise; it's naturally very tempting but I would like to take some time to think it over, and I would like to see the contract you have in mind, in black and white. But, should I see fit to accept it, it would only be on the basis that any form of sexual harassment would be perfectly adequate grounds for breaking it—that would be a specific clause I would insert, Mr Goodman, and that would also be non-negotiable.'

He grimaced and said softly, 'You're angry, Briony.'

'I am truly angry, Mr Goodman, I freely admit it,' she replied mockingly. 'May I also offer you some advice while we're on the subject? On your next mistress-acquiring jaunt, stay away from any references to their punching washing machines; it tends to stick in one's craw—indeed *any* references to what strange creatures they can be. And both blackmail and bribery go down well with fewer women than you would imagine, believe it or not! As does the practising of deception and masquerading at being what you're *not*. Another thing you should be aware of: the facts of life may not be pretty but to have them rammed home to one—and again I freely admit you were right about some things, it has been a...lonely year— but to have them rammed home to one the way you've done it, to be propositioned and taken advantage of the way you've done it, not only leaves one feeling degraded but feeling like taking a sharp instrument to you.'

She stopped and waited although not sure for what. Mirth? Mockery... She was destined to be surprised. He stood up at last, his eyes entirely enigmatic and he said thoughtfully, 'Well said, Briony. I apologise for the washing machine, incidentally.'

Her lips parted and she frowned bewilderedly. 'Do you mean...were you *still* testing me out?' she gasped then. 'I don't believe you!'

He smiled fleetingly and said with some irony, 'Which would you prefer?'

'I...I...what *is* all this about?' she stammered.

He took his time answering. Time he spent allowing his hazel gaze to drift over her expressionlessly, from her pale face and the circles of weariness starting to show under her eyes, to her tense, incredulous stance, the lovely riot of her sun-streaked hair, then he shrugged slightly.

'Something you'll see as a further misrepresentation, no doubt,' he said finally. 'But unfortunately Nick Semple...' he paused as her eyes dilated ' ...is married to a cousin of mine, although how long they'll stay married is a matter for conjecture. But not only is she a cousin of mine, she was reared by my parents when her parents were killed in an accident so I look upon her as a sister of sorts. Further to complicate the issue, Briony, and in case you've ever wondered why you ran into the storm you did, my family has been a silent partner in the Semple operation for years; so much so that they rather depend on my— goodwill to be able to continue. Now I must tell you that I don't hold much brief for Nick but that's something entirely between himself and Angelique, not *three* people as you may have thought.'

Briony opened and closed her mouth several times but couldn't speak.

He waited with courteous attention then said, 'On the other hand, you have surprised me, Briony. You're certainly not quite what I expected, and you express the sentiments of a—let's say, more intelligent, moral sort of person than a lot of the Semples led me to believe, but then they have a bit to lose, unfortunately. So I think it would be advantageous if we were to get to the bottom of it, although I think we should defer it—you look to be out on your feet.'

Briony swallowed and found her voice was still strangely useless, which gave him the opportunity to continue.

'On the subject of the advice you offered me, you were, of course, right.' He grimaced. But then he said with all the old amusement and irony, 'None of that changes the fact that I would like to go to bed with you, or make love to you, or have sex with you, or whatever you like to call it. It's strange, isn't it, how two people attract each other and there's not a damn thing you can do about it?'

Briony found her voice at last. '*Do* about it?' she said in an oddly strangled way.

'I refer, naturally,' he said gravely, 'to one's thought processes, which just don't seem to be as governable as one would sometimes like. But then again, between two *unattached* people who find themselves subject to these thought processes despite all else—well, who's to say what could happen?'

'I can say—will you get out?'

'Just going, Briony,' he responded lightly. 'That's the second time you've commanded me to disappear; I hope it's not going to become a habit.' His eyes laughed at her. 'Why don't you take yourself to bed? Things might appear in a better light tomorrow.' And with a careless little salute he walked past her, making no attempt to touch her, and let himself out.

CHAPTER FOUR

As EVERYONE left the ten o'clock meeting briskly the next morning, Briony was conscious of two things: that her job would be easier from now on and that she was obviously the subject of some speculation among the staff.

Why the second should be was not difficult to analyse. Her manner, when she'd introduced Grant Goodman, had been, despite her best effort, constrained. Nor had she looked her best. And then of course both Linda and Peter Marsden could testify, and might have, even if involuntarily in Linda's case, that things weren't running exactly smoothly between her and the new owner.

Why her job should be easier was even simpler to analyse. Grant Goodman had been quietly impressive. He had made his plans for Heath House known to them and she'd seen the excitement this had generated. He'd outlined concisely their areas of excellence and the few areas where he felt they could improve. He'd assured them that he had no plans to sack anyone at this stage but let them know that in the long run only their individual performances would guarantee employment. And the overall picture had been plain to see, much as it annoyed Briony. She had a backstop now, in other words, but it was more—there was a man at the helm, a man not to be trifled with, moreover, and she knew that, unfair as it seemed, things would be easier to run because of it.

'Well, what would you like to do now?' she heard herself say brightly as they were left alone in the dining-room.

Grant Goodman surveyed her in silence for a moment. He wore jeans and a green sweater and it had not diminished his laid-back air of authority by so much as an inch. He also looked as if he'd been striding through the cold morning air just before coming to the meeting; his eyes were alert although his thick tawny hair was ruffled and the overall impression was one of honed physical fitness and a man who could handle anything.

By contrast she felt dull and jaded, and her slim grey skirt and plain white wool jacket, both impeccable and designed to make her look managerial, made her feel drab and colourless instead.

'Are you unwell?' he asked abruptly.

She coloured and framed the words to tell him it was none of his business but stopped herself. 'No.'

'Then you didn't sleep very well, if at all.'

She bit her lip. 'I was...overtired, probably. That's all.'

'I'm not surprised. Take the day off, Briony—how many days do you take off, incidentally?'

'I...it varies,' she said stiffly.

'I wonder. You wouldn't be so foolish as to imagine you can do without any breaks, would you?'

There was no amusement or irony in his eyes, she saw, just something rather grimly impatient. 'No,' she said stiffly and turned away. 'Very well. But first of all I should —— '

'There's only one thing you need do,' he broke in, 'and that's inform Linda you're not to be disturbed. If she has any problems she can come to me. Off you go. Even if it gives you the time to cry your heart out at the unfairness of life, it will probably help.'

Briony drew an angry breath but as he eyed her steadily she changed her mind, swung on her heel and left him.

And ten minutes later she closed herself into her suite, leant back against the door and battled a desire to do just that—cry her heart out. But, although successful, it was a battle that left her feeling more exhausted, and she kicked off her shoes, left a trail of her clothes on the way through to her bedroom, where she wrapped herself in her tartan robe and put herself to bed.

The surprising thing was that she slept, although not dreamlessly. Nick Semple's dark good looks intruded in a chilling little dream that woke her once, but she was so thankful Angelique hadn't appeared that she went back to sleep. It was two o'clock in the afternoon when she finally stirred, stretched and sat up.

There was some weak sunshine playing through her window but the day had grown colder. She got up and lit her stove and took a long, leisurely spa. Then she dressed in slim navy ski pants and a Fair Isle sweater, made herself a sandwich and sat down to write her weekly letter to her mother. But it struck her as she wrote that she felt more guilty than

usual about the fact that she'd left Sydney
without barely an explanation to her mother,
whom she admired and loved dearly and who
had thought so much of her daughters that
she hadn't even considered marrying again
while they were growing up, out of respect for
their grief for their father. Yet she'd heard no
word of complaint from her mother about this
precipitous move that had taken her so far
away, and she sometimes thought her mother
was the only person who really understood her
motivations and the sometimes ungovernable
ambition that moved her. And she thought
briefly of pouring it all out in this letter.

Unfortunately, as she wrote, because her
ears were attuned to every little nuance of
Heath House, she started up automatically a
few times at an alien sound only to sink back
with a grimace, and then decided it wasn't the
best time to be looking deep into her heart.
She spent the rest of the afternoon tidying her
drawers and going through her clothes but
with another question on her mind—whether
to go or stay. Where to go if she did leave
Heath House, for example. And how to
stay...

At six-thirty her phone rang and it was Linda. 'Briony,' she said cautiously, 'I've a message for you.'

'Go ahead, Linda.'

'Uh—Mr Goodman presents his compliments and requests that you have dinner with him in his chalet.'

It was like a flash of lightning through her brain, the speed with which she thought. 'Thank you, Linda,' she said easily, 'but could you tell Mr Goodman that I've already arranged to have dinner with a friend at Cradle Mountain Lodge?'

'Briony,' Linda said uneasily, 'I don't think that's wise, nor is it true—you've had no calls inward or outgoing all day.'

'Linda—is he actually spying on my phone calls?' Briony asked ominously.

'No! Of course not but *I* just couldn't help noticing ——'

'My dear, much as I value your alertness in all matters ——' Briony paused then said less abrasively, 'Stay out of this, Linda. Please.'

'But ——'

'And I'm just about to make a phone call, Linda.'

'But ——'

'And you can tell him if you like, if it makes you feel better, that I do have a friend at Cradle Mountain Lodge—she's the head housekeeper and we go way back.'

'Oh, Briony,' Linda said in hurt tones.

Briony winced. 'Look, I'm sorry,' she said. 'Thank you for trying to be a friend—but truly, it's best if you just stay out of it.' And she put the phone down quietly.

It was a clear, starlit, freezing night as she drove back to Heath House from Cradle Mountain Lodge. It was also close to midnight—she'd stumbled into a staff party at the lodge and been only too happy to take advantage of it. She was happy to notice that Grant Goodman's chalet was in darkness.

That gives me at least eight hours before I need to tangle with him again, she thought, as she put her car away quietly. I wonder what I can come up with in eight hours?

As it was it turned out to be one of *those* days. Wet and cold, not that that was so unusual but it always meant more pressure on staff when guests couldn't get out and about. Oh, for an indoor heated pool and squash court, she caught herself thinking longingly once. But it was the series of other problems that cropped up that really tested her. A guest with a severe asthma attack at six o'clock in the morning; an elderly couple truculently convinced they'd been robbed of two hundred dollars, which had required the most diligent search of their room to find that they'd hidden the money in a tissue box on their arrival and forgotten they'd done it; a blocked toilet in one chalet and a mysteriously broken window in another; a waitress dropping a tray of six full soup plates over several guests at lunch.

'I don't believe it,' Briony said to Linda after she'd helped clear up the mess and soothed everyone down. 'I still don't understand how they came to break that window.'

'Honeymooners,' Linda said succinctly.

Briony raised an enquiring eyebrow. 'Does that follow?'

'You'd be surprised what honeymooners get up to, Briony,' Linda said virtuously.

'Indeed I would not, but I'd never heard of the event that can make the earth move actually shattering windows! No matter,' she said as Linda laughed, 'surely nothing else can go wrong today!'

Linda's laughter turned to a grimace. 'Have you seen Mr Goodman this morning?'

'Only in the distance, thank heavens. How did he take my—defection last night?'

'On the chin, like a man,' Grant Goodman drawled from behind her and strolled into the office behind Reception.

Linda turned bright red but Briony merely clenched her fists.

'I gather you two have had quite a morning,' he added casually, and sat down on a corner of Linda's desk.

'If you were listening —— ' Briony stopped and bit her lip.

'I was, quite unintentionally,' he replied guilelessly. 'I'd stopped to inspect the register on my way in. Who are these honeymooners for whom the earth moves so cataclysmically, by the way?'

Linda blushed even more brightly and Grant Goodman took pity on her. 'Don't answer,' he said lightly and touched one finger to her hot cheek, causing Linda to look up at him with a certain light of hero-worship in her eyes.

You poor, foolish kid, Briony thought irritably. 'Can we do anything for you, Mr Goodman?' she said.

He stood up. 'Well, Briony, I was hoping you could. I had the plans for the new buildings flown in this morning, which is why I haven't been much in evidence. I picked them up from the airstrip. So what I was wondering was this—if you have no prior engagements, no dates with friends or anything else to do, could you meet me in my chalet in an hour, to inspect them?'

Briony's eyes glowed a hot, bright blue but she said equitably, 'Certainly, Mr Goodman. I'll be there.'

Linda swallowed and sighed heavily as she watched his retreating back. But as Briony turned to her convulsively she said, 'I'm not saying a word!' And proceeded to say several. 'But after all your hard work, now, when things are really rolling like this and you could be part of it—it just doesn't make sense, Briony!'

'It may not to you,' Briony replied shortly, 'but—oh, hell!' She rubbed her brow. 'Perhaps you're right.'

*　　*　　*

'What do you think?'

'I think they're excellent on the whole.' Briony stared at the blueprints, then round the chalet a little disorientatedly. Each chalet was two-storeyed with an open-plan living area, including kitchen and dining, downstairs, and the sleeping area and spa upstairs beneath a sloping roof. This one was decorated in shades of soft blue and green, was pine-panelled, thickly carpeted and luxurious despite his ambitions to make it more so, and the wood stove was burning merrily. They were sitting at the dining-table.

'Only on the whole?' he prompted.

'It's not that easy to visualise things from a plan but one thing that does occur to me is that it's also not that easy to service an extra building like this from one central kitchen in another building. You've planned for a coffee shop and snack bar beside the pool but I can't see any kitchen.'

He looked at her thoughtfully. 'That was the idea, one central kitchen, but perhaps you're right. Does it not complicate things, though? Two chefs, two sets of freezers, et cetera, et cetera.'

'I don't think so. You're going to have to increase the kitchen staff anyway and from my experience of chefs they prefer their own domains so it would be better to put a short-order chef in charge of this operation, in his own domain.'

'Mmm... That sounds sensible,' he said slowly, 'so long as a lot of doubling up of ordering and wastage and so on doesn't go on.'

'Trust me,' Briony murmured. 'With good supervision —— ' She stopped abruptly.

'So you're going to stay on,' Grant Goodman said into the silence.

Briony got up and walked over to the window. It was raining heavily. 'I haven't made up my mind.'

'You said —— '

'That was a slip of the tongue.'

'Tell me your reasons for not staying on, Briony.'

She turned from the depressing view and sighed. 'I should have thought they were obvious but, in case not, take the fact that we are fast becoming an ''item'' among the staff, for starters. You saw fit to have a go at me in front of Linda just a little while back, you ——'

'And from what I heard,' he said mildly, 'you had already discussed our situation with Linda so any—dissemination seemed pointless.'

'No, I hadn't, not actually,' Briony defended, but it sounded uneasy even to her own ears. 'All right! Before I ever knew who you were, I . . . I . . .'

'Made your dislike of me obvious to Linda,' he supplied.

'*Yes*. Which was unfortunate as it's turned out but no crime. And really only unfortunate in the sense that Linda is an intensely curious but warm-hearted person and she's— worried about me. That doesn't,' she said with more than a trace of irony, 'alter the fact that she obviously views you as the Great Panjandrum and God's gift to women rolled into one. But I would never . . . do anything to denigrate you in front of other staff,' she added stiffly.

'What about Chef Marsden, the other night?'

Briony grimaced. 'I was in a state of shock then, I'm afraid. You'll have to forgive me for that one.'

'Well, if you're not about to denounce me as a blackmailer and a womaniser to all and sundry——' a mocking little glint lit his eyes '——I don't see why we couldn't contrive to "de-itemise" ourselves. I would be happy to contribute more than my share.'

'Does that mean...?' Briony stared at him. 'Have you changed your mind?'

He raised an eyebrow at her and shuffled the blueprints together. 'About us in a personal context? No.'

'Then I don't see how we could hose down the speculation,' she said baldly, 'because we are still going to be at considerable loggerheads.'

He shrugged, rolled the plans up and put an elastic band around them. 'I thought a period of peace and quiet might help you to see things in a different light, Briony. Am I to take it you don't plan to confide in me about Nick Semple?'

'Look—what if I were to tell you the Semples were right? That I...stalked him, that I blackmailed him, that I was actually

caught in the act of kissing him by his wife—
what then? You can't tell me you would still
want to go to bed with me or make love to
me or have sex with me or whatever you call
it!'

'Sit down, Briony, before you burst a blood
vessel,' he said drily. 'What *are* you telling
me?'

Briony sat because her legs felt a bit shaky.
'This,' she said hoarsely. 'While you may feel
it has something to do with you because she's
your cousin, I don't feel *I* have anything to
do with you at all. But despite all that it's
over. It's been over for twelve months! Nick
Semple is quite safe from me now and you
don't have to vent any of your—lack of
goodwill on him. The blame,' she said
steadily, 'was mine.'

'Look at me,' he commanded quietly but
when she did her eyes were blue and blank
and his own eyes narrowed. 'Why are you
protecting Nick, Briony?'

She looked away. 'I've nothing more to say,
Mr Goodman. Well, except this. I've already
made one bad mistake in my life. To...enter
into a relationship with you, such as the kind
you've outlined...' she paused and clasped

her hands on the table '...would be adding cynicism to injury,' she said barely audibly. 'Even if it's not your idea of helping me to expiate my sins,' she added with a sudden, knife-like glance. 'No, I think I'm much better off soldiering on alone, thank you all the same.'

'Do you still love him?'

'No.'

'Did you ever love him?'

'No.'

'What kind of relationship would you like to enter into with a man, Briony?'

She sketched a smile. 'As a reformed ex-fortune-huntress and breaker-up of marriages who got her fingers badly burnt? Let me see... I don't really know,' she said wearily. 'Look, could we have a break?'

'OK,' he said obligingly, 'but just let me say this. I don't go in for any kind of expiations through sex. I much prefer the normal, mutual-pleasure variety that can apparently even shatter windows, although I've never reached quite that—er—height.' He smiled wryly.

Briony closed her eyes.

'I would also like to say that I don't altogether believe you, which may have something to do with the fact that I still find myself attracted to you. And may,' he said with sudden cool, 'have something to do with the fact that I know Nick Semple rather well. But by all means let's have a short break in hostilities.'

She opened her eyes and said before she could stop herself, 'Don't you believe in love and marriage any more?'

Their gazes locked. 'Do you?' he asked.

'I...I...forget it.' She shrugged.

'Why did you ask me, then?' he queried.

She looked away and traced a meaningless pattern on the table with her fingertip. 'Well, if you must know I suppose it helps to know what makes people tick if you can know their philosophies.'

'I agree with you,' he said drily. 'That's why I'd really like to get to the bottom of yours. But in the hope that this may help you to work out what makes me tick—I went through some years of love, so-called, and marriage, mainly because there were two children involved——'

'Two...' Briony stared at him.

'Twins, actually, or one *set* of children, but none the less. And so, while I wouldn't rule out marriage categorically...' He paused and shrugged as he said, 'It's a little hard to visualise.'

'What are they? The twins.'

He studied her meditatively before he said, 'A boy and a girl. They're twelve.'

'So now,' Briony murmured, 'you believe in drowning your sorrows in a series of women.'

'No,' he replied curtly. 'I would rather abstain than do that. But the ideal, to my mind, since it all happened—yes, it would be to share a steady, worthwhile relationship with one woman who could be happy that way. Who valued her freedom too, was career-minded and——'

'And heaven help her if she fell in love with you,' Briony said huskily. 'What if she became imbued with the desire to have children? I'm told most women are subject to it.'

'Are you trying to tell me that's beginning to bother you, Briony?'

'No. If I'm trying to tell you anything it's that—do you know what I think would suit you best, Mr Goodman? A divorcee with her own children and similar disenchantments. I don't think our "battered" illusions do quite match up, in other words.'

'So you still cherish love and romance, Briony? That surprises me.' He lifted an amused eyebrow at her.

'Has anyone told you you're insufferably smug?' she said softly.

He grimaced. 'Here we go again. Are we about to come to blows? Because if so it is time to take a break.'

'I——' But a knock sounded on the door.

It was Linda, looking really worried. 'I'm sorry to disturb you but the Reynoldses are convinced they've lost their son.'

Both Briony and Grant Goodman stared at her. 'Lost? How?' Grant Goodman said.

'He went for a walk about two hours ago. He said he wasn't going far and they're now convinced he's fallen down a cliff.'

'For a walk? In this weather! How old is he?' Briony asked.

'Sixteen—you know, the family that arrived this morning from Darwin.'

'Darwin,' Briony muttered of that city at the opposite end of Australia and about as opposite in climate as could be. 'He'll freeze. Get Lucien and John, Linda. Uh—ask them to come here as well as the parents—if you don't mind, Mr Goodman,' she said perfunctorily. 'We don't want to alarm people unnecessarily.'

'No. Go ahead. It isn't Friday the thirteenth and I don't know about it, is it?'

Half an hour later, Briony said, 'This is a waste of manpower.' She wore yellow oilskins and a similar hat which was dripping as the rain came down steadily. Visibility was restricted to a few feet often as patchy fog swirled around them. The trunks of the trees were black and sepulchral and no self-respecting bird was to be heard. The track was squelchy underfoot.

'It's not, you know,' Grant Goodman replied. 'It's common sense. Were we to lose you we'd be in double trouble.'

'I know this track like the back of my hand,' Briony said tartly.

'Besides which,' he went on imperturbably, 'if the kid has sprained an ankle or broken a leg, you would be of little help to him.'

Briony compressed her lips then cupped her hands to her mouth and called, 'Robert! Are you there?' There was no sound. 'They should be shot, letting him out on his own in this. On his first day and only wearing a plastic raincoat!'

'Agreed. But that's not going to help young Robert now. Let's just concentrate on finding him.'

Briony shot him an angry glance. 'Why do you always make me act like a monster?' she said through her teeth.

'It's probably something to do with your suppressed rage towards me,' he replied. 'I mean, it sort of vents itself on—well, anyone to hand but particularly anyone who is giving you a hard time,' he said wryly. 'It's also a well-known syndrome. When Dad berates Mum, she berates the kids and they kick the cat.'

Briony made a disgusted sound. 'You could be absolutely right,' she retorted. 'I wonder if men realise how often they start that chain of useless events? *Robert*!'

They climbed steadily for half an hour. 'I hope to God Lucien or John is having more luck,' Briony said anxiously.

'Mmm... I'm glad you alerted the ranger station too. The more people to fan out in this, the better—stop,' Grant Goodman said with quiet intensity and closed a hand over her wrist.

It was a minute before she heard it and then it was a thin, muffled cry for help coming from a ravine to their right. 'That's him. Hang on, Robert!' Briony called. 'We're coming!'

It took them a good twenty minutes to clamber down the side of the ravine to where the frightened sixteen-year-old was lodged between a tree and a boulder, shivering desperately, and his first words were, 'I got lost and fell but I think I can walk with someone to help me—I've done something to my hamstring, that's all; I know because I've done it before playing football but I feel so stupid and I'm *freezing*!'

'Are you all right?'

'Fine,' Briony whispered as she stripped off her oilskins, then looked around dazedly. 'Oh, sorry, we're back in your chalet—I'll go —— '

'Don't be ridiculous,' Grant Goodman said roughly. 'You've half carried a hulking teenage front row forward down a bloody mountain. You're going to be the next one in need of first aid!'

'Well, it was better than letting him die of hypothermia, because the two-way radio chose today to pack up,' Briony responded and, to her horror, started to cry. 'If it isn't Friday the thirteenth it certainly deserves to be,' she wept.

Grant Goodman stared at her grimly then he said something beneath his breath and strode over to her and took her in his arms. 'Don't—just don't fight me,' he warned. 'You're about the most stubborn woman I've ever met, but quite the bravest.' And he swung her up and took her over to the settee in front of the fire and sat down with her still in his arms. But there was no fight left in Briony. She cried into his shoulder unrestrainedly until he smoothed the wet strands of her hair from her face and said quietly, 'Stop now, it's over.'

She had all but stopped when Linda again knocked on the door. Grant Goodman made no effort to change their positions as Linda came in but looked at her questioningly over Briony's head.

What Linda made of things Briony was destined not to know immediately because she had her reactions well under control by the time she came into view and perched on the edge of the chair opposite. 'He's going to be fine, Robert is,' she said reassuringly. 'The doctor's checked him over and is staying with him for a bit longer just in case; there is a slight strain to his hamstring but he'll get over the cold. We've packed him up with electric blankets and so on.' She stopped, her eyes resting anxiously on Briony.

'She's going to be fine too,' Grant said. 'This is just reaction and exhaustion. I'll look after her. Could you present Chef with my compliments once again, Linda, and ask him if we could have dinner here in about an hour?' He grimaced and added, 'This is becoming a habit. Could you also bring some clean, warm clothes for Briony? And I think it would be a good idea to respond to any enquiries with the simple truth. People are bound to be aware that some emergency has occurred and it might deter others from taking risks like it—but the kid feels foolish enough as it is, so——'

'I will handle it all with great diplomacy!' Linda said eagerly. 'You can rely on me, Mr Goodman.'

He smiled at her. 'I know we can, Linda.'

Briony spoke for the first time only after Linda had closed the door behind her. She said shakily, 'You do realise there's a serious case of hero-worship in the making there?' And fresh tears started to roll down her cheeks.

He studied her for a moment then said gravely, 'Would you like me to get the doctor to look you over, Briony, while he's here?'

She tensed and attempted to sit up. 'No! I don't —— '

'Well, then here's your alternative. I'm going to put you in the spa while I make us a drink. We can discuss things like hero-worship later.'

CHAPTER FIVE

'I CAN do this,' Briony said unsteadily as he set her down on her feet in the bathroom and activated the spa.

He turned to her and raised an eyebrow. 'I wasn't proposing to be as hackneyed as that.'

'As what?' She frowned at him.

His lips twisted. 'As what you had in mind, dear Briony. Undressing you with my own hands—that kind of thing.'

She swayed slightly and ran her hand through her damp hair. 'I must have got it wrong. You did say, didn't you, that you were going to put me in the spa?'

'Another day, perhaps,' he murmured. 'But it's good to see some of your usual spirit returning. Don't fall asleep and don't lock the door—I'll check you in about twenty minutes. But I'll give you plenty of warning.'

Briony closed her eyes and turned away.

In twenty minutes, she was out of the spa and wrapped in a towel when he knocked. 'If you've got my clothes just leave them outside the door, thanks,' she called.

'Are you decent?' he called back.

'Yes, but barely so—uh——' The door swung open.

'Well, if you wouldn't mind dressing in the bedroom,' Grant Goodman said politely, 'I could do with a spa myself.'

Briony clutched the dark green towel closer and said through her teeth, 'Aren't we straying into hackneyed territory now?'

'Not at all,' he replied wryly but made no pretence of not looking her up and down, from her bare creamy shoulders to the long, naked and still glistening wet sweep of her legs beneath the towel. 'I'm merely cold, damp and dishevelled.'

'This was *your* idea!'

'So it was. Let's just say I couldn't help myself,' he said gravely while his hazel eyes were wickedly amused, 'so it mightn't be an idea to stand there too long, Briony, in case I'm tempted to persuade you to come back in and join me.' And, so saying, he pulled his sweater and shirt over his head together.

She went with a delicate flush staining her cheeks, but not before she'd been unable to avoid the view of his long, powerful, tanned back.

There was a small bag of clothes on the bed. She pulled out Linda's selection—a pair of black ski pants and a black fine angora sweater, underwear, lacy white socks and her black velvet flatties. Why black? she wondered as she dressed swiftly. Not that black didn't suit her but she couldn't help thinking it was an odd choice on Linda's behalf. Then she chided herself for being fanciful, found her hairbrush, did what she could with the tangle of curls, and took herself downstairs just before the bathroom door opened.

There was a tray of drinks set out and a small platter of canapés. She raised an eyebrow, stood lost in thought for a few minutes as she contemplated just walking away from Grant Goodman's chalet, then it was too late. He came down the stairs and by a strange coincidence was dressed all in black himself, in a thick black sweater and black cords.

They stared at each other and then even Briony had to smile. 'Twins,' she said huskily, 'but you have to thank Linda for my attire.'

'And Linda has another talent,' he said, reaching the bottom step. 'You look desirable in anything but black becomes you beautifully.'

'I don't know, it made me think of funerals—my funeral perhaps,' she murmured as he came right up to her. 'Because I'm about to give in my notice, Mr Goodman.'

'Oh, no, you're not, Briony,' he contradicted, and he was so close she could see the greeny flecks in his eyes and breathe in the scent of warm, clean male flesh. And she was assailed by the memory of his strength as they'd brought Robert down the mountain, his strength, his patience and his quiet persistence when both she and Robert had been stretched almost beyond endurance, and she was assailed by the paradoxes that made up Grant Goodman. The way he used words like a rapier at times, the way he'd cut her out and subjected her to all he had, but for all that was a man you had to admire and know you could depend on. No, she thought, with a distressed little jolt of breath, no, please, don't do that to me...

'Not until we've done this at least,' he went on evenly. 'I've spared the hackneyed; I'm not

about to spare you honesty. Such as this...'
His arms closed around her and he claimed
her mouth before she could say a word.

And when he finished kissing her she
couldn't leave the circle of his arms. Her face
was flushed, her breathing erratic, her mouth
bruised and her eyes large and dark with the
knowledge that being kissed by Grant
Goodman filled her with desire and a
dangerous rapture, and there was no way to
hide it from him...

'So,' he said barely audibly, moving his
hands to her waist, 'we've been caught doing
this before. Which is to say that dinner is due
to descend on us any minute. Let's—compose
ourselves a little, Briony, lest we join the ranks
of certain athletic honeymooners on the
gossip scale.' He let her go but ran his fingers
through her hair and smiled slightly. 'What
do you think?'

'You asked me what I thought.' Briony
pushed away her plate. Once again she'd
failed to do justice to Chef Marsden's culinary
genius although she had eaten half a fillet
steak and had finished her soup.

'Mmm.' He reached for her glass and poured in the Moorilla '89. 'Drink it,' he murmured. 'We were destined to have this wine whether we liked it or not.'

She sipped it with a little shrug. 'So we were. It's very nice.'

'It is, isn't it?' He sat back. 'Tell me your thoughts.'

She drew a pattern on the tablecloth with a clean fork, her eyes on it, her hair falling forward. 'Why won't you just accept my resignation and let me go?' She dropped the fork, looked fleetingly across at him and raised her hands to push back her hair.

'Several reasons. To get a combination of the managerial expertise and local knowledge you have wouldn't be easy —— '

'It wouldn't be that difficult,' she said with a trace of scorn that she hoped masked the flicker of hurt she'd felt. 'I had no local knowledge when I came here.'

'Ah, but you came here determined to bury yourself away. You were also unencumbered, except with memories. It's always a problem to find people to come to the more remote places, and to keep them,' he said significantly, 'particularly if they have husbands or wives and children.'

'It's not that remote,' she said, but felt as if she was clutching at straws. 'It's only an hour or so from Launceston.'

'Be that as it may—neither Launceston nor Hobart is exactly a metropolis, with all due respect to Tasmania. And here, you're at the bottom of a mountain in the middle of a National Park full of them. That would drive a lot of people crazy as a permanent lifestyle.'

Briony returned to her fork drawing. 'Go on.'

'And then there's the fact that I wouldn't like to do you out of a job.'

She smiled but not at him. 'That's a little hard to believe.'

'I don't see why it should be. I've offered you excellent terms and I haven't pinned you to my bed with a gun to your head. In fact the two occasions we've indulged our mutual attraction have been—revelations, you might say. Why don't you just relax and go with the flow, Briony?'

She jumped up and said intensely, '*No*. Because it might as well be a loaded gun!'

He pushed his hands into his pockets and observed her thoughtfully. 'I know what you're afraid of. That you won't be able to help yourself —— '

'Yes, I *will*.'

He shrugged and looked amused. 'As you did earlier?'

She blushed, picked up her wine and stared stormily into its ruby depths. 'You're a...' She tightened her mouth.

'And you are eminently kissable,' he said softly. 'Moreover, you enjoyed it —— '

'You said yourself I was probably starved of... not for food.'

'So any man could wring that kind of response from you? My dear Briony, I fully understand your urge to insult me but you're wasting your time. You're also insulting yourself, not to mention fooling yourself, if you really believe that.'

'Oh?' She looked up and across into his eyes. 'Who's to say I'm not like your wife who had the soul of a tramp? Who's to say you don't have a predilection for women like that?'

The silence lengthened between them and she had the satisfaction of seeing his eyes go grim and hard. 'And who is to say,' he said in a voice she barely recognised, 'you're not simply a termagent with a beautiful body, one of those overbearing women who can't bear to accept anything from a man they can't dominate? Take care, Briony,' he warned with cold, precise insolence, 'you might find yourself taking to jackboots one day in your bid to ride roughshod over men.'

She gasped, went white and opened her mouth but he said coolly, 'You can go now. I'll see you in the morning.'

It was only the physical excesses of the day that saw her sleep that night. In fact when she got back to her suite she was reeling with tiredness and a brainstorm of emotional turbulence—so much so that she felt she only had two choices: go to sleep or go mad. And, although her weary muscles were much improved when she got up, the emotional turbulence was not, nor was it helped by Linda, who was in a chatty mood when they sat down together in the office after breakfast.

'I rang a friend of mine in Sydney last night, Briony,' she commenced the conversation, quite pointedly staying away from any reference to what she'd witnessed in Grant

Goodman's chalet the day before—or so Briony thought.

'Good for you.'

'She's also in the hotel business and she's a mine of information. Apparently it's common knowledge over there that Grant Goodman has gone into the resort business. Did you know—— ' she glanced at Briony speculatively '—that he's been behind the Semples for years?'

'I was probably the only one who didn't, Linda,' Briony said drily, and reached for the next week's menus. 'Did you have a good gossip about me at the same time?'

'No,' Linda said resolutely. 'I had already heard the story anyway but I prefer to make my own judgements. I also regard you as a friend so I wouldn't gossip about you.'

Briony looked up with a twisted little smile. 'You're a honey, Linda, actually, and I don't know why you put up with me.'

Linda put her head to one side and grimaced. 'That's what friends do. I also did something else. I got all the background info on Grant Goodman for you.'

Briony's hands stilled and her smile faded. 'What do you mean?'

'About his marriage. I thought it might help.' Linda contrived to look both wise and motherly.

Briony stared at her and couldn't for the life of her think of a thing to say.

'It was a disaster by all accounts. Do you know who he married? No...? Lisa Bairnsdale.'

'Oh...'

'Yes.' Linda nodded with particular significance. '*That* Lisa Bairnsdale. Now, you have to admit she's enough to turn any man's head. Did you see her in the last movie she made? Wasn't she wonderful? But the story goes that she is one tough lady underneath, that she's had liaisons,' Linda said delicately, 'all over the *world*, that her father spoiled her atrociously—he was the mining magnate——'

'I know,' Briony said.

'And she once said to someone——' Linda lowered her voice and looked around '——the only real man she's ever had was Grant Goodman, because he was the only man who ever said no to her.'

Briony clasped her hands to her mouth for a moment; she couldn't say why. 'Well,' she spoke hastily then, 'thank you, Linda, for all that but how come your friend is such an expert on...them?'

'It's not exactly a secret, although I think they play it down because of her image. But Cynthia is one of those mad movie buffs as well as a Lisa Bairnsdale fan and apparently,' Linda said confidentially, '*he* got custody of the children, so he must be a good father. And he protects their privacy fiercely.'

'I'm sure he does. I'm not sure if I get the point of all this,' Briony said slowly.

'Has *he* told you any of this?'

'No—well, not in any detail.'

Linda nodded sagely. 'It can only help to know a bit about a man, can't it? For example, if I had known that Lucien, our Alpine guide extrordinaire, was also an extra-ordinary flirt, I might not have...well, I would not have,' Linda said severely.

Briony had to smile feebly. 'Do you think anything you've told me guarantees Grant Goodman is...different?'

'He must be. They wouldn't have given him custody of his children otherwise.' The phone beside Linda rang at this point and she picked it up and said into it, 'Reception, may I help you . . . ? Yes, Mr Goodman, she's right here. Yes, I'll tell her.'

Briony raised an eyebrow at her.

'He wants to see you on the site of the new building right away. He doesn't sound in a very good mood—Briony, what have you done?'

'I may have put the slightest dent in his ego, Linda, that's all,' Briony replied, standing up. 'I'm sure he'll find a way of retaliating.'

It was a fine day although the ground was still damp, but everything sparkled and the haunting perfume of lemon thyme was strong in the air. Grant Goodman was not alone and he introduced Briony to the two men with him, an architect and a builder whom he'd had flown in and picked up from the airstrip himself. He gave no appearance, unless you knew him, of being anything other than brisk and businesslike. But he tested Briony intently on summer aspects and winter aspects, prevailing winds and any existing drainage problems they might have which could affect the new site. Then he dismissed her and told her he would see her in the office at two when he would like to go over their food- and alcohol-ordering procedures with her.

'Your people have already done that,' she was unwise enough to say.

'I always like to see these things for myself,' he replied coolly, and turned away.

What was to turn out to be the only bright spot of the morning was the departure before lunch of Dwight and Dora and friends. Briony made a point of farewelling them and was besieged with invitations to visit them in Chicago, and when Grant Goodman happened to chance by on his way to deliver the architect and the builder back to the airstrip Dwight buttonholed him and made a little speech.

'I'd like to wish you a whole lot of good luck with Heath House, Grant, and it's been a real pleasure to meet you. Thank you for telling us you're the new owner and telling us about all your plans. We sure will give the place an almighty plug back in the States! But don't you forget what I said once before; this little lady here —— ' he put an affectionate arm about Briony '—is the best darn thing that ever happened to the place. So you see you take good care of her—it wouldn't be the same without her!'

*   *   *

'I've got all the records out, invoices et cetera, right back to day one,' Briony said colourlessly, as Grant Goodman closed the door of the office at two o'clock precisely.

'Thanks,' he said briefly, and sat down on the other side of her desk. 'You don't accept any kickbacks, do you, Briony?'

She stared at him stonily. 'If you mean do I accept any bribes for ordering from this wholesaler or that, no, I do *not*.'

He ignored this. 'And you don't cream off the odd bottle of Scotch, carton of cigarettes, roll of toilet paper or box of tissues—anything like that?'

She compressed her lips.

'Or lift the odd sheet, pillowcase, blanket, towel or tablecloth for your glory box?' he persisted.

'How dare you?' she said stormily.

'I dare——' he sat back '——because it happens a lot, as you very well know. Why are you so upset? Because I'm treating you purely like an employee?' He lifted a mocking eyebrow at her. 'Or did Dwight's little speech go to your head?'

'It did not,' she said with a white shade around her mouth. 'And if this is how you treat managerial employees you're going to find them even harder to come by than you might have thought——'

'All the same, things do disappear,' he said gently. 'Towels, ashtrays——'

'Oh, I've known far stranger objects disappear, Mr Goodman. One couple we had cleaned out every light bulb in their chalet. If you searched everyone's luggage as they left you'd be amazed at the number of our towels you'd find, but this can't be news to you and you'll find the incidence of it here no higher than normal.'

'Good. Because when guests steal or "souvenir," as we all know they do, there's not much we can do about it. When the staff get in on the act, unfair as it may seem, it's your job to police it. And to set a good example.'

'You're welcome to search my rooms, Mr Goodman!'

'Thank you but I'll take your word for it, Briony.'

She couldn't help it—for the life of her she just couldn't help it. 'I knew men had fragile egos,' she said bitterly, 'but your lack of resilience leaves me virtually speechless.'

'Ah.' He played with a pen pensively for a moment then lifted his hazel eyes to hers. 'I take it you're referring to our last clash of words? It wasn't my ego you wounded so much as my discovery that you are not only stubborn, which is all right, but a liar, which is definitely not, and —— '

'Don't go on. I must warn you I also have a temper and that I've restrained myself where you're concerned, but there's a limit! I really don't care whether you see me as stubborn or a termagent but I am not a *liar.*'

'No?' he said idly. 'Then why won't you admit that what you and I do to each other started from the moment we laid eyes on each other, is virtually ungovernable when we're in each other's arms, and is entirely different from what you're so determined to label it as?'

Briony took a jerky breath. 'What would you like me to admit it is? Love? How could I end up other than hurt again if I did?' She stopped abruptly then tried desperately to cover her tracks. 'Why didn't you tell me you were married to Lisa Bairnsdale?'

His eyes narrowed. 'I don't see what that's got to do with it,' he said drily. 'It doesn't alter the fact that I got taken for a flat, for all that she may be the best in the business. It's no consolation to me, believe me.'

'I didn't mean that,' Briony said huskily.

'What did you mean?'

'I . . .' Why did I even say it? she wondered helplessly. Simply to cloud the issue. 'She— there could be reasons for her being the way she . . . is.'

'There could be—there are.' He shrugged. 'She has this free artistic spirit, she was unbelievably indulged. But the simple fact is, I don't know if any man can change her, but I do know I couldn't and I stopped wanting to a long time ago.'

'By all accounts,' Briony said involuntarily, 'she admires you for that.'

He looked amused. 'You're very well-informed suddenly, Briony. How come?'

She blushed fierily. 'It wasn't me, it was . . . It doesn't matter.'

'Let me guess. Our Linda?'

Briony refused to reply.

He laughed softly. 'Dear me, we haven't been able to "de-itemise" ourselves yet, apparently. But look, if you are curious, even with Linda's connivance, the one thing I can't deny is that we had two children together and I can't deny *them* their mother, but that is the sole contact we have—or want. Both of us. It's over. You know,' he said slowly, 'great physical beauty is never enough on its own. I looked for more in Lisa and couldn't find it—apart from all the other diversions.' He grimaced. 'And she obviously didn't find what she was looking for in me. Perhaps it was just as simple as that.'

'And what if you don't find what you're looking for in me?' Briony whispered.

'The way we're going,' he said flatly, 'we're destined never to know, aren't we?'

'But what——' Briony stopped momentarily '——hope would there be for us even if we did find—anything?'

He stared at her dispassionately. 'What did you have in mind? Marriage, Briony?'

She fought back sudden tears. 'Even for someone with my record...' She shook her head. 'Forget it.'

'You're afraid of getting hurt,' he said sombrely. 'Are you really, Briony? Or is marriage the ultimate stake you play for? Is that why you won't even countenance what I've offered?'

She got her tears under control. 'Probably,' she said harshly. 'Pity—you have to be a much bigger catch than Nick Semple—that's two that got away! Never mind. There'll be others.'

They stared at each other then Briony jumped slightly as there was a knock on the door and she called out to come in in a slightly cracked voice. It was young Robert, still hobbling rather painfully but otherwise over his ordeal with the resilience of youth.

'Hi!' he said. 'I was looking for you two. Mum and Dad wanted me to come and apologise for being such a dreadful nuisance—I mean, I wanted to apologise too—' He broke off looking red-faced and frustrated.

Grant grinned at him. 'We know what you mean, old man. Sit down and tell us how you feel.'

Robert sat eagerly. 'Oh, I'm as fit as a fiddle except for this hamstring. I just feel so darn stupid!'

'Don't,' Grant said. 'We all make mistakes, but so long as you learn from them you're pretty well all right. Is that not so, Briony?'

'It usually works that way,' she said after the barest hesitation, and smiled at Robert. 'Your Mum and Dad reckon you're a pretty hot footballer.'

'It's my life,' Robert replied simply, then grimaced. 'At least, it used to be but I'm wondering now if I wouldn't like to be a National Parks ranger. Is it very hard to get into it, Miss Richards? I think I'd like to work right here at Cradle Mountain.' And he looked at Briony with all the unconscious fervour of a sixteen-year-old in love.

Briony blinked, glanced at Grant, was horrified to see his eyes full of wicked amusement, and said uncertainly, 'Not that hard, Robert. But you'd be a very long way from home...'

Robert waved one hand grandly. 'Mum and Dad are always saying they can't wait to get us all off their hands,' he said as if that solved that.

Briony swallowed. 'Well, mums and dads say those things but they're generally teasing you. Uh—aren't there any National Parks around Darwin.'

'I suppose so,' Robert said vaguely. 'But it wouldn't be the same.' He stopped and then, to his obvious horror, started to blush as if he had suddenly realised how he'd given himself away.

It was Grant who came to his rescue. 'I'd say it would be a pretty fine career for someone who's really athletic and wouldn't like to be shut up in an office all day.'

Robert turned to him thankfully. 'That's just what I was thinking, Mr Goodman!'

'Well, how much more school have you got to do?'

Robert's face fell. 'About eighteen months.'

'Then that will give you plenty of time to look into it. I would imagine the Visitor Information Centre would be able to give you all the requirements. Why don't you go down and see them?'

'I will. Yes, I will. Anyway——' he stood up '——thanks a million for rescuing me. Can I... could I write to you? To both of you,' he said hastily. 'Just to let you know how I'm going. Seeing as you saved my life.'

'I think we'd be delighted to hear from you, Robert,' Grant said, and stood up and held out his hand. 'But if it hadn't been us, someone else would have saved you, I'm sure.'

'Don't *laugh*,' Briony warned as the door closed behind young Robert.

But he did. 'You get them in at all ages, obviously, Briony.'

She tightened her mouth and cast him a look that contained a mixture of sheer frustration laced with despair.

He sobered. 'Do you get the feeling this war of words has gone on long enough? I certainly have the feeling it's degenerated into a slanging match as a cover-up for what you really feel.'

She gestured sharply. 'A moment ago *you* were accusing me of getting a kid of sixteen "in".'

'Mmm... All right, so I'm not pure and lily-white myself when it comes to trading insults. I may even be suffering from a slightly fragile ego.' He smiled, but unamusedly. 'As you put it earlier. But at least I can admit why we are the way we are. I want you, Briony. My reason, my instinct both tell me that we are uniquely matched—for that. They also tell me that despite your protestations to the contrary you can't get it out of your mind, because it's as if there's a force between us that we can't deny. Believe me, this doesn't happen often, not with this intensity between two people. Have you ever known it before?'

The silence was complete for a minute. She couldn't tear her gaze away from his and she couldn't drag her mind away from the truth—she was dangerously attracted to this man. Even when she was angry with him and convinced she despised him she couldn't help but know she was fuelling her enmity along to counter that ever-growing fascination with him as a man and even as an enemy. Just to look at him was to remember how she felt in his arms, how her body responded to his... But, she thought dully, what happens to a woman who falls in love with a man and can only ever be his mistress?

She took a shaky little breath and looked away. 'It could never work,' she said flatly.

He said nothing for a long moment, then, with no inflexion, 'I've had a slight change of plan; I'm going to Hobart for a few days. By the way, you'll be happy to know Frank Carter's operation was successful.'

She looked back at him and flinched inwardly as she encountered his merciless hazel gaze. He added, 'I'll be at the Sheraton if you need to get in touch with me.' And he left.

CHAPTER SIX

GRANT was away for four days.

The weather was beautiful during that time and no crises cropped up although the fact that they were full was a burden in itself. But Briony was thankful and she strained every nerve to ensure that Heath House ran like clockwork. On the afternoon of the fourth day, she caught a glimpse of herself in a mirror, was shocked to see that she actually looked haggard and decided to take a couple of hours off.

Linda was embarrassingly in agreement with her. 'Do it before you drop,' she said sternly. 'I can hold the fort. Where are you going?'

'I just thought I'd take a ramble along Truganini's Track, nothing strenuous.'

'Good idea. Go before you change your mind!'

Truganini, named after the last Tasmanian Aborigine, skirted Lake Dove on the eastern side towards Cradle Mountain and was definitely a soft walk. But Briony had no objections to that as she strolled along breathing in the beauty of the scenery and feeling the warmth of the sun. But she got no further than a quarter of the way down it when Cradle Mountain did one of its notorious about-faces weatherwise. Clouds started to scud across the sky and a cold, sharp breeze got up to ruffle the deep blue waters of Lake Dove. There were a lot of walkers about but as Briony soldiered on they were all going in the opposite direction, back to the car park. She stopped once to pull a parka and fleecy-lined leggings from her pack and knew that even if it snowed she couldn't go back to Heath House yet. It didn't snow but it got colder and colder and as she lengthened her stride it added unfairly and quite ridiculously to her sense of frustration and despair. Even the weather's against me, she thought, and tried to laugh but found herself crying instead.

That was how Grant Goodman found her, leaning against a tree weeping silently with her eyes closed.

'Briony—don't.' He put out his hand and touched her wet face lightly.

Her lashes flew up and her lips parted. 'You!' she gasped. 'What are you doing here?'

'I came to look for you.' His eyes were sombre and probing. 'Has this storm of emotion anything to do with—us?'

'Us?' she whispered, feeling dizzy as she realised the kind of hunger she'd battened down while he'd been gone but could no longer deny, faced with the tall, strong lines of his body, the lines and angles of his face. 'Us,' she repeated desolately. 'There is no such thing.'

'Yes, there is. Why do you think I'm here, looking for you?'

'To ask me to be your mistress again?' She shook her head wearily and brushed at her eyes impatiently. 'I can't —— '

'Forget about that,' he said brusquely and put his hands on her waist. 'I'm asking you only one thing—is it a torment to you . . . not to be my lover? It is to me.'

Briony rocked slightly beneath his hands and her eyes were full of shadows as she stared up into his. 'A torment?' she said huskily, but knew suddenly that there was no dissemination she could offer that would deceive him now, no way she could hide her soul from that penetrating hazel gaze, or hide how, even through her parka, she was trembling at the feel of his hands on her. 'It's like a living hell,' she said despairingly, 'but——'

'It needn't be. Don't.' He put a finger to her lips and drew her into his arms. 'If I start kissing you now I'm liable not to be able to stop,' he said barely audibly. 'We could also freeze—will you come with me?'

She could only nod against his shoulder.

His chalet was warm and welcoming—it was dark and stormy outside by the time they got back but the housekeeping staff had done their job well. The fire was lit, the curtains closed, lamps on and the bed turned down, no doubt, she thought with a tremor.

They'd said little on the walk and then drive back but had been deeply aware of each other so that words had seemed unnecessary. Or is it that I just don't have the strength to say what I should say? she wondered, and pulled off her parka.

'I better give Linda a call,' she murmured, and bit her lip.

'I will.' He did, and told Linda briefly that she was back but would be off duty for the rest of the evening. 'Did you note that I didn't order dinner?' he said with a crooked little smile, coming over to her. 'I hope you're not hungry.' And he took her face in his hands. 'You look so... strained. Is it any help if I tell you that *I* have ridden roughshod over everyone I've come into contact with in the last four days, so much so that the name of Goodman is now mud in Tasmania?'

Her lips trembled into a shaky smile. 'We make a good pair but —— ' she sobered '—I don't know why. For all you know I am everything the Semples said about me.'

'And for all you know I am a blackmailer and everything you ever thought of me. But I think the fact is there's something in you and something in me that's irresistibly drawn to the other, and whatever else we are doesn't seem to change it. Let me demonstrate.'

She made a husky little sound of protest but he stilled it unanswerably. And when he'd finished kissing her he picked her up and took her upstairs.

He set her down in the middle of the room but kept her in his arms. 'Is there anything you want to say?'

Briony stared up at him and wondered if she should tell him the truth about herself. But some instinct prompted her not to, some instinct for self-preservation, she was to realise later. 'No,' she said barely audibly. 'I think you're right.'

His eyes narrowed and he traced the outline of her mouth. 'There's one thing I don't believe in,' he said gently. 'Any sense of constraint felt by one party or the other.'

She lowered her lashes and rested against him. 'Constraint? I *would* be lying if I told you you're forcing me to do this against my will, although I don't know about my better judgement. So I can't...tell you...how I'm going to feel afterwards. But right now ——' she lifted her face to his and her lips trembled into a smile although her eyes were honest but wary '——you make me feel alive as I haven't for a long time; you fill me with a kind of rapture that is rather devastating and ——'

She got no further. He kissed her more deeply than she'd ever been kissed and she responded freely and couldn't still the answering joy she felt at the brief intensity that flowed through his body before he seemed deliberately to take hold and slow the pace. And as he took her clothes off item by item he did things to her she'd never experienced. He explored every part of her body as he freed it with a touch that was gentle yet ravaged her senses, taking them to heights she'd never known. He took all the time in the world to make sure she was participating freely and with pleasure in this act that she'd been so afraid of admitting was inevitable between them. He made her skin feel like warm satin as it glowed like ivory in the lamplight, her breasts heavy with longing and her nipples almost unbearably sensitive. He made her waist feel slim and fragile beneath the spread of his hands and the curve of her hips like perfect fruit. And his body was a delight to her, strong and heavily muscled but perfectly proportioned and lithe.

There then remained the one area of her he hadn't explored and she gasped as his long, sensitive fingers made the last contact with the utmost delicacy—gasped not because she was unready but because he had made sure she was trembling on the brink, and warm and wet with the need to welcome him into her body.

Their gazes caught and held; she saw that he knew what he had done to her and she made no attempt to hide the momentousness of it and, for a moment, he held her very close before moving his weight on to her—and she could have died for him in that moment.

'Briony?'

'Mmm...?'

'I thought you were humming.'

'Was I?' She blushed and hid her face in his shoulder.

'Is there any reason why you shouldn't?' He ran his fingers through her hair. 'I can't think of one.'

'Do you know many people who...wake up humming?' she asked ruefully.

He tilted her chin so that he could look into her eyes and considered gravely. 'Not one. You're—unique. How do you feel?'

The delicate colour returned to her cheeks. 'I think I might have given myself away there already,' she replied, seeking for some composure but unable to hide what was in her eyes.

He stared at her and there was an oddly intent glint in his eyes, as if he was studying something that puzzled him, then it was gone as she started to look wary. 'I don't know about you,' he said, kissing the tip of her nose, 'but I'm starving.'

'If we were in my suite I could make you a snack —— ' She broke off and bit her lip and then began to feel hot and cold as she thought of the implications of this act, because there would be no way to hide it . . .

'Briony.' He stilled her convulsive movement and gathered her naked body close, and read her mind with devastating accuracy. 'There's not a thing we can do about it.'

'But . . . I *hate* the thought of everyone knowing and exchanging knowing looks behind my back.'

He grimaced and that little glint was back for a second but he said drily, 'If you think I welcome it, you're wrong, but —— '

'You . . .' She stopped.

'But,' he said firmly, 'it really has nothing to do with anyone else. We're two adults who made this decision; it's unfortunate we're so publicly placed at the moment, but I promise you no one will treat you with less respect than you deserve because of it.'

'How can you promise that?' she whispered.

'Because we're not going to go out of our way to flaunt it or cheapen it in front of people, which is our own best defence, and because they'll have me to contend with if they do.'

Briony shivered. 'I don't like being in that position; I —— '

'I'm sure you don't, my brave warrior,' he said with a smile at the back of his eyes and his hands caressing her hips, 'but I don't see an alternative. Do you?'

And that was when it really hit her—that she'd given herself hostage to this man who had made love to her in a way she could never forget, but not only that. He had somehow stilled her doubts about him and, despite the fact that she knew he must doubt her morals, had drawn from her the warm, sensuous heart of her femininity... I was so afraid of this, she thought with a tremor. I can't love half-heartedly—does he have any idea what that means? And there's one doubt he hasn't stilled: where will this lead?

'Grant,' she said huskily. 'I —— '

'That's the first time you haven't called me Mr Goodman,' he said wryly.

She winced and he sobered. 'Go on.'

'I think I should tell you about Nick Semple. I ——'

'No, I don't think you should now, Briony,' he said evenly and his hands stilled. 'I don't think it has anything to do with this. I don't think it can change the way you made love to me; it certainly can't change the way you affect me. I think things have gone beyond that.'

'I see,' she said on a breath, and she did. 'So we are to be lovers, and that's all?'

'No,' he said steadily, and his hands started to move on her body again. 'Friends as well.'

She closed her eyes. If you cry, Briony, she warned, I'll never forgive you. You knew all along how it had to be; he's never deceived you and he might have good reason to be like this but his will and his sheer attraction was too strong, and what do they say about hope springing eternal? Oh, God! She clenched her teeth as a flash of pain ran through her with the thought that to find a man like Grant Goodman, whom she could have loved if he'd been anything but what he was, whom she couldn't help herself loving anyway, was almost unbearable. But what do I do now? Put a brave face on it . . .

'Briony?'

She lifted her lashes, felt his body stirring against hers and felt the immediate answering hunger in her own. 'Yes...?'

His gaze wandered over her face, which was a little pale now, and the luxurious disorder of her hair, the shadows in her eyes. And he closed his eyes briefly and said with sudden savagery, 'I shouldn't have ——'

'No,' she said with sudden calm and smoothed her palm along his shoulder, 'I was as much to blame. And you're right, we're adults, we're hurting no one else—let's just leave it at that. I thought you said you were hungry?' Her lips quivered into a smile but she veiled her eyes from him.

'Briony, I would give—anything to make you wake up humming again, can you believe that?'

Her lashes fluttered up and she saw him staring down at her as if what he saw hurt him, and the tears she'd denied suddenly sparkled on them. 'W-would you?' she stammered. 'I mean—I'm not...I understand, but...'

'Yes, God help me, I would,' he said very softly and kissed her eyelids. 'Don't cry. I——'

But she stopped him. 'I won't. I—won't.'

Contrary to her fears, she was not subject to knowing looks the next day although she had no doubt that everyone knew. Not that she'd spent the night with Grant Goodman, but he had, later, gone to the kitchen himself and collected a snack for them and he had walked her to her suite just before midnight. And, although they hadn't even held hands and he'd merely delivered her to her door, she was an old enough hand in the business to know that neither of these events, nor the length of time she'd spent in his chalet, would go unnoticed by *someone*.

But what puzzled her was their reaction. Certainly Lucien looked at her the next morning with a tinge of regret but everyone else treated her with a curious gentleness. They went out of their way to make things easier for her, they plied her with tea and coffee, a special tray of morning and afternoon tea began appearing, complete with some freshly baked delicacy, whereas normally she took those breaks on the run. Linda bestowed on her the special benediction of asking her absolutely nothing and covering for her when she lost track of what she was doing. They brought things to her that normally she would have gone looking for, such as the news that the new lot of lobsters were full of meat and much fresher, that the store of firewood was going down a bit quicker than anticipated and so on. In general they treated her with so much care, concern and consideration that she was quite startled and unable to help mentioning it to Grant when it turned out to be not a lapse that only lasted a few hours.

He looked at her wryly. 'I don't think it's so surprising. They admire and respect you.'

'But they're treating me as if I'm an invalid!'

He took her hand and pulled her down beside him; it was three days after he'd first made love to her and they'd just dined separately, she with a new group of guests and he alone in his chalet, which was a reflection of how they'd spent the last days, she working as normal and he working on the new building project and not coming together until after dinner. But it was a pattern that was disturbing her increasingly, and not only because just catching a glimpse of Grant was sufficient to make all her nerve-ends tingle but also because it seemed like setting the groundwork for a new way of life.

She'd lain awake last night after he'd left her, beset by two sets of thoughts—one concerning this pattern that was being laid and another which took her a while to get into order because it had started out as a new disenchantment with her work. And she'd had to needle at the roots of it to trace its cause, which had come as stunning little revelation. The disenchantment was to do with her surroundings, she'd first realised, and then come to see that it was because they were not her own; in fact, she had very little of her own around her. She'd always lived in other people's places and, although her rooms in Heath House were pretty and comfortable, other people had made them so and she'd added virtually nothing.

She'd clenched her fists as the implications, once the first mystery was solved, had rolled in on her... She was thinking of a home; she was thinking beneath the tumult of becoming Grant Goodman's lover, in terms of her personality creating a unique place, and she knew this meant much more than bricks and mortar. She was thinking, in other words, she acknowledged with pain, of a place to share with a husband and, one day, children, and there was nothing she could do to stop herself; it was probably the destiny of most women, and it crept up on you—it invaded your mind when you were in love and it was as simple as that.

Thus she'd tried, in the darkness, to talk sense to herself. She'd pointed out that she'd always thought of herself essentially as a career woman, that she could possibly go mad with nothing but babies and housework to occupy her, that she'd always assumed if she did marry she would still be able to work— without giving it a great deal of thought. She'd even once thought, not very seriously although it came back to her now with a stabbing sense of irony, that she would make a good wife for a rich man who needed someone to entertain for him a lot and with a couple of estates she could run like clockwork.

And when she'd thought this she'd tried to set her mind deliberately on another course. Did it always have to be like this? for example.

Could she not spend time with him elsewhere, times and places where there was no work and they could be together all day and all night? Perhaps they could fly into places where no one knew them and take holidays together. Would he ever allow her to meet his children . . . ?

She remembered the thought that had intruded somehow with an inward shiver as Grant took her in his arms on her settee in front of the fire after dinner. 'Not an invalid,' he said quietly. 'There's something about you at the moment that would affect a stone.'

She lay against him. 'I suppose you have to take the credit for that,' she said at last.

He kissed the top of her head. 'No. Well, only a little.'

'I think you're being modest.'

He sounded amused as he said, 'I'm trying to be but the fact is it's like working with pure gold.'

'That's a curious analogy,' she said slowly and lifted her head to look into his eyes. 'What do you mean?'

He narrowed his eyes and didn't try to explain. He said instead, 'Have I offended you?'

'I don't know... Well, I do,' she amended and grimaced. 'It's not terribly flattering to be compared to working a metal, however precious.'

'My mistake,' he said gravely. 'What I meant was, making love to you and making you look like this is not only my doing, it's already there in you. It's honest joy and honest giving.'

Briony caught her breath. 'Does it really show?' she whispered, then bit her lip. 'I mean——'

He touched her face lightly but his eyes were suddenly unreadable. 'You told me once I made you feel alive; that shows and——'

But she said quickly, 'And the edges have softened, probably. I am glad I don't look as if I could go about punching washing machines any more.' She extricated herself with a little grin, went over to the fire and added a couple of logs.

He watched her as she bent gracefully then straightened and the slender flow of her back, waist and thighs was clearly visible through the soft ivory wool of the dress she wore. And when she turned and their eyes met, as suddenly as she'd been unable to read them before she could see what was in them now.

'Grant,' she said a little huskily, 'I don't ——'

But he stood up and came over to her before she could finish although he didn't attempt to touch her. 'I could go now if you wanted. Is that what you want, Briony?'

She licked her lips and was tempted to tell him of all her lonely thoughts the previous night but she said, quite foolishly, 'Go? Without making love? I mean...' And she blinked several times to hide her confusion because what she'd seen in his eyes had told her he wanted her in the most specific way.

'If you're not in the mood...'

'It's not that I'm not in the mood, but ——'

He smiled slightly and changed the subject. 'Can you get off tomorrow morning?'

Her eyes widened. 'I suppose so. Why?'

'Would you like to climb Marions with me from the Lake Dove side, weather permitting?'

'Yes...'

'Then that's what we'll do. Goodnight, my dear.' And he left quietly.

Briony sank down into a chair as the door closed and tried to deal with several things. A sense of shock and bewilderment, a sense of loss that was almost physical, an understanding that she'd just witnessed an iron will being exercised and—a warning? she wondered dazedly. That I have to do things on his terms or not at all? But I have and I am, something cried out within her, in spite of the fact that it goes against the grain with me and in spite of the fact that although everyone's treating me so well I would rather not *be* in this position. What more does he want? That I never tell him my inner thoughts? That all I accept and offer is the physical side of love?

She put her hands to her mouth and couldn't help herself thinking about the physical side of love with Grant Goodman. *All*, she reflected and closed her eyes as she was shaken by a storm of longing. That's how I got into this position; I don't seem to be able to resist him. How can a man who affects me like this...? But she couldn't formulate things any more and her cheeks grew hot and her eyes curiously distracted as she thought of the things Grant Goodman did do to her, how he could make her senses soar and her body flower and her heart overflow...

With love? she thought, because she could no longer avoid it. And, How could I be this way except with a man I loved?

She got up and roamed around restlessly, recalling that she'd thought she'd been in love twice before, only to find that differing expectations had taken the bloom off both affairs and left her wary and disillusioned about giving herself to a man the way she seemed to be made to do it. But neither of those affairs had contained all the elements she shared with Grant Goodman. The passion, the heights she hadn't believed possible, the way she was so totally at his mercy when he handled her body, then the tenderness as he brought her down from those heights, and finally the lovely aftermath of lying in his arms, spent and drowsy and just talking idly until she became afraid of going to sleep...

'Afraid of going to sleep.' She said the words aloud and hugged herself because they seemed to say it all. 'I might have been better as an established mistress,' she also said aloud and with soft bitterness. 'Would I mind spending a full night with him here then? Am

I making stupid distinctions? God knows, I need to make a stand about something—don't I? Or is it too late? No. If I can't tell him how I really feel, if I'm to be frozen out of everything but his bed, I have to make some kind of a stand...'

'Why Lake Dove side?' she queried the next morning as she drove her own car. Lucien was taking a party along the Lake Rodway track.

'It's more of a challenge,' Grant said idly. They'd met for the first time after breakfast and she'd tried to be perfectly normal when she'd driven round to his chalet to pick him up. At the same time she'd asked herself how you could be perfectly normal with a man who knew you as intimately as he did now and probably knew you were back in fighting mode. Their gazes had clashed as soon as they'd laid eyes on each other and he'd raised a wry eyebrow but said nothing.

'It's that all right,' she replied. 'It's not the best of days either, but so long as it doesn't rain we should be all right.' It was a brisk, chilly but bright day.

'We can always turn round and go back, Briony,' he pointed out mildly.

'No.' She tried to match her tone to his and even managed to smile faintly. But she added with an underlying steeliness she couldn't help, 'I'm committed to Marions now.'

'That sounds almost ominous.'

'Why do you say that?' She pulled up in the car park.

'It just...' he paused and looked into her blue eyes thoughtfully '...made me wonder what would happen to us if our commitments ran in opposite directions.'

Briony returned his gaze steadily. 'I don't think we're into the business of commitment, Grant, so it may not be a problem. Are you ready?'

'Yes.'

They climbed steadily side by side and he offered her no help, which she would have scorned anyway, and it was exhilarating and strenuous. They stopped a couple of times but didn't say much and she resolutely concentrated on what her feet were doing to take her mind off the ease with which Grant climbed; she was determined to match him step for step. It was a small triumph, although she could not say why, when she reached the summit a couple of minutes ahead of him.

'Well done.' He came to stand beside her as she scanned the wonderful view, so clear in the bright, cold air.

'Thank you.' She pulled off her pack and donned her parka. 'I've brought us something to eat and drink.' And she knelt down to unpack a small thermos of coffee and cold roast beef sandwiches.

'And I brought this.' He knelt down beside her and produced a silver flask from his pack. 'Brandy. You can have it neat or in your coffee.'

'Oh, in my coffee, I think,' she said brightly. 'Who knows what I might do otherwise?'

'Something like this?' he murmured, and drew her to her feet. 'Lose your head and kiss me?' he suggested.

'Not this morning, Grant——'

'Yes, this morning, Briony. For one thing, I won't be here tomorrow morning.'

Her lips parted and her eyes widened. 'Why?' she whispered. 'Is it over already...?'

'No. Unless you want it to be.' But he said no more until he'd kissed her thoroughly and made her acutely aware that her body now knew his and all the trauma she felt couldn't change that knowledge. 'Shall we sit down?' he said finally but kept her in his arms a moment more.

She nodded and couldn't help wondering where her earlier aggression had flown to.

They sat in the shelter of a rocky outcrop and it was he who poured the coffee and laced it with brandy but it wasn't until she'd eaten a sandwich that tasted like sawdust and sipped some coffee that he said, 'Tell me what you wanted to say last night, Briony.'

She hesitated. 'Would you tell me first why you would like to know now when you didn't then?'

'Sometimes it's better not to say things in the heat of the moment. That's a philosophy I've often found it wise to pursue. So it seemed to me that a period of reflection was called for. But I couldn't help knowing you were—unhappy.'

She sipped some more coffee. 'I have the feeling I might not be cut out for this, Grant,' she said barely audibly.

'There is an alternative. You could move to Sydney; I'm sure you could find a nine-to-five job, and whenever I'm in town, which is frequently, we——'

'Don't go on.' She was amazed at the steadiness of her voice but some of her resolution of the night before came unexpectedly to her aid. 'That wouldn't suit me at all.'

'What would suit you?'

'I don't know.' She laid her head back against the rock and stared into the sky and was again possessed by disbelief that a man who could make her want him so fiercely at times could say what he had. 'I suppose I do believe that I'm not just—well, a body. Surely there must be more to it than that?'

'There could be. We don't have to make Heath House the only place we ever meet. I'm due in Melbourne for a meeting of the Cattlemen's Union in a fortnight's time, for example. *You* are violently overdue for a break from the wilds of Tassie and anyway, you have leave due to you now. We could have five days there—I'll only be spending two days at the most at the meeting and the rest of the time we could spend doing what we liked. Have you yearned at all for some shows, some culture, some bright lights, some up-market shopping, some small, intimate, different ethnic restaurants?'

Briony caught her breath. 'Bookshops,' she said huskily. 'Music shops...oh...'

He picked up her hand and threaded his long fingers through hers. 'Will you come?'

She lowered her gaze from the sky at last and looked into his eyes, and was shaken by the memory of the last time she'd lain in his arms. 'I...yes.'

He pressed her fingers then raised her hand to his mouth and kissed the back of it gently. 'I'm leaving this morning.'

Her fingers clenched. 'Why?'

'I got a message last night that Lisa, who was to have Scott and Hannah for their half-term holiday, has been held up overseas.'

'Before or —— ?' She bit her lip.

'After I left you.'

She was silent for a moment. 'Scott and Hannah—your children?'

'Yes.'

'And they're at boarding-school?'

'Uh-huh. Quite happily.' He grimaced. 'I gave them the option of day school or boarding—they both made the same choice.'

'Where will you take them? For their holiday?'

'To my mother. She still lives on one of the cattle stations. She adores them, they adore her, they love the life up there and I've promised to teach both of them the rudiments of sharp shooting.'

'Do they—look like you?'

'It's funny—they're not identical but Scott takes after Lisa while Hannah is more of a Goodman. I'm sorry I'm leaving so—out of the blue.'

'So am I——' Briony broke off and blushed. 'You must think that's strange after the things I said earlier.'

He released her hand and traced the hot colour in her cheek but he said curiously sombrely, 'Actually I don't because I have to tell you honestly that I—would like nothing better than to take you with me. It's going to be a long, hard haul until I can make love to you again.' And he took her face in his hands and kissed her lingeringly.

They made good time getting down Marions but once at the car he surprised her again when he told her to drop him off at the airstrip.

She looked at him bemusedly. 'You're flying out?'

'Yes. I've chartered a plane to Launceston then I'll take a commercial flight to Sydney. There's a bit of fine timing involved—I'd like to be there to pick them up from school. Linda has sent my luggage down to the airstrip.'

'You needn't...you shouldn't have worried about Marions, then.'

He smiled down at her and made her go weak at the knees. 'Oh, yes, I should. I needed that time with you.'

CHAPTER SEVEN

THE fortnight passed at times with frightening speed and at times at a snail's pace. But two things remained constant—a yearning to be with Grant Goodman but also the dilemma as to whether she was doing the right thing. And if she did go, how should she be? Would she have the strength to take any kind of a stand? And why, at the back of her mind, was she increasingly perturbed by the fact that he no longer wanted to hear about Nick Semple...?

Then she was in Melbourne, in an exquisite suite in a luxury hotel with a bowl of red roses to welcome her and a note from Grant to say that he would be joining her at six-thirty in the evening and would she care to dine with him in style?

Briony stared down at it, lost in some most intimate memories for a moment. Then she calculated that she had about six hours and she set to work. Her first stop was the hotel beauty shop where she had her hair trimmed

164

and pampered, a facial and a manicure and stocked up on cosmetics. Then, feeling like a new person and smelling deliciously fragrant, she went shopping for clothes.

He arrived at six thirty-five and for a moment they just stared at each other across the room. He had on a conservative dark suit that made him look distinguished but a little unfamiliar and she wore a black silk dress moulded to her figure with one shoulder-strap and the other shoulder bare. Her hair gleamed and caught the light, a riot of curls but shaped now into a shoulder-length bob. Her lips were painted a shimmering deep berry-red and she wore a pair of drop gold and pearl earrings, her only jewellery.

'You look—stunning,' he said at last, and held out his hand.

'Thank you,' she murmured, and went into his arms.

'This—might not be a good idea,' he said barely audibly, staring down into her eyes.

Her lips trembled at the corners. 'I thought of waiting but I couldn't resist dressing up for you—if that's what you mean?'

He ran his hands along the warm, smooth bare skin of her shoulders and arms. 'That's what I mean. But I think I'll have to be strong because I wouldn't have missed you dressing up for me for the world.'

'You could kiss me, though,' she offered with a mischievous glint in her blue eyes. 'Lipstick can always come off and be put on again.'

'Is that a fact ?'

'Mmm . . .' She raised her arms around his neck. He slid his hands down to her hips and complied.

It was some minutes later when they were sitting side by side on an elegant sofa, holding hands, that he said, 'How have you been?'

She laid her head back. 'Busy. They've dug the foundations.'

'I meant—otherwise.'

Briony hesitated. Then she said honestly, 'Restless, somewhat bereft but able to restrain myself from punching washing machines.'

He laughed.

'How was your holiday with the children?'

'Pretty good. Well, *somewhat* complicated by the fact that Hannah is a natural shot and Scott is not. But I've lived through it before. She also outrides and outswims him. In some ways she reminds me of you, a very athletic...girl.'

Briony grimaced. 'Poor Scott. I hope he has other areas of excellence to compensate.'

'Fortunately he's brilliant at school.'

They were silent for a time until he said, 'We should go.'

She turned her head and there was something wry and humorous in her eyes although she said demurely, 'We should indeed, Mr Goodman.'

'On the other hand we could always have dinner here,' he countered with an answering glint in his eye.

'It was your idea to go out, however,' she commented.

'One of my less than brilliant ideas, I'm beginning to think, Briony.'

'Not at all.' She released her hand and stood up. 'Do you dance?'

'Yes.'

'Well, I had this hope that you would be taking me somewhere where we could dance. Or go on somewhere. It seems a lifetime since I did that.'

He studied her gravely, still lying back lazily on the settee, and her heart started to do strange things as that clever hazel gaze roamed up and down her, lingered on the shadowed sheen of her legs through a pair of black patterned tights below the short skirt of her dress. Then he stood up. 'Very well,' he murmured, putting his hands on her waist. 'In about one minute.' And he started to kiss her throat, her shoulders, and the silk of her dress might have been non-existent as his hands moved upwards to cup her breasts.

It was barely longer than a minute when he released her but her breathing was ragged and she felt flushed and dishevelled, but not only that—aching for him unbelievably. 'That wasn't—fair,' she whispered and licked her lips.

He smiled slightly. 'They say all's fair in circumstances like these. If you go and repair the damage, although to my mind you look wonderful, I'll ring down for a car.'

They ate asparagus vinaigrette, Atlantic salmon with a hollandaise sauce and pavlova garnished with strawberries and kiwi fruit. The restaurant was decidedly upmarket and all the women were beautifully groomed; diamonds flashed discreetly and many a mink jacket lay carelessly over the back of a chair. The service was excellent and the food delicious yet Briony found herself feeling distracted and uneasy.

It wasn't the lack of a diamond or two or a fur—she never worried about those symbols of wealth and status and, indeed, she'd drawn some admiring glances when they'd arrived—so had Grant. It was, she decided, because they'd shared some minutes of warmth and communication sitting side by side on the settee but since seemed to be back on an exposed plateau, metaphorically speaking. A place where her nerves were jangling and there was a tangible air of constraint between them although she knew that if he suggested they go straight back to the hotel she would do so. Is this physical thing so strong between us, she wondered, that we can't be comfortable in each other's company until it's been appeased?

'Ready?'

She glanced at him through her lashes. 'To dance?'

'Yes.'

'Do you really want to? I mean . . .' She bit her lip.

'Changed your mind, Briony?'

'I thought you might have. We . . .' She faltered. 'We don't seem to be on the same wavelength any more,' she finished, and winced because that was so palpably untrue in one respect at least.

'I think we are,' he said drily, then picked up her hand as an unmistakable look of hurt touched her eyes. 'I'm sorry. We could dance another night.'

'All right.'

'Grant . . .'

'Mmm . . . ?' He lifted his head from her breasts.

'I . . . I . . . don't know. Nothing . . .'

'Have you any idea what a problem this has been for me?' He was lying beside her, and he propped his head on one hand and drew the other slowly down her body.

She shivered and drew one leg up but didn't answer and he went on presently, 'That's what happened tonight. But in fact I meant to make you feel the opposite—not withdrawn and unhappy.'

Her lips twisted. 'This doesn't seem to be very withdrawn,' she said huskily.

'All the same, you are.'

'How...how do you know that?' she said on an indrawn breath.

'I've made love to you before—remember?'

'Of course,' she whispered, and trembled.

'So, the fact of the matter is, I could no more have danced with you tonight than I could have flown to the moon. I just didn't realise it would mean so much to you.'

'It doesn't,' she said swiftly. 'I only said it in the first place to—well, tease you a little and because I haven't danced for ages, but,' she said with a wry sort of honesty, 'now it looks as if I was playing hard to get. And what—frightened me was that suddenly ——' her voice dropped and her eyes were shadowed and confused '—we were like enemies again and it was nerve-racking and —— '

'Don't go on.' He cupped her cheek and kissed her gently on the lips. 'I should be shot for making you feel like that but it was only a measure of how much I wanted you.'

Her lips curved. 'Wanted?'

'Present, past and future tense. Can you doubt it?' He eased his weight on to her, slid his arms round her and buried his face in her hair. 'Could you also take pity on a poor besotted fool who has been dreaming of this for a fortnight and not only at night?'

She did.

They lay together afterwards, at peace at last, not saying much but in each other's arms and she with her head nestled in his shoulder.

'What's on tomorrow?' she asked once.

'Cattlemen and their problems,' he said ruefully, 'but that's the last of it. I should be free by four.'

'That's all right. I haven't attacked the bookshops yet.'

'What did you do today?'

'Oh, clothes,' she said dreamily, 'after a stint in the beauty shop. It was heaven.'

'Am I to take it you have more than that black dress in store for me?'

She kissed the long, strong column of his throat. 'I have one that's altogether strapless and backless.'

He groaned. 'I mightn't survive it.'

She laughed.

They were quiet for a time until he said, 'Sleepy?'

'Mmm...'

'Goodnight, then.' And he kissed the top of her head.

'Goodnight.' She yawned. 'I'm so glad I don't have to be afraid of falling asleep,' she said drowsily, and tensed despite being on the edge of sleep.

'What now?' he queried quietly.

'Nothing.'

He didn't pursue it and she fell asleep in his arms.

He was up before her and he woke her with breakfast on a trolley.

Briony pushed her hair back and sat up convulsively, blinking dazedly. Then she realised she wore nothing and pulled the sheet up.

Grant sat down beside her, looking amused. 'You're in Melbourne, you're with me and have the whole day to do nothing if you want to.' He wore well-pressed grey trousers, a crisp white shirt and a navy tie.

Briony lay back against the pillows. 'I thought I must have overslept! What is the time?'

'About eight-thirty ——'

'I *have* over ——'

'No, you haven't,' he contradicted. 'You're on holiday, remember? And I only woke you because I didn't want to leave without— saying hello.'

'Oh.' Her lips curved. 'That was a nice thought. Thanks.'

'Actually I wanted to do more than *say* hello,' he commented.

'Did you, now?' she replied innocently.

'Despite your confusion you're in a very good mood, Briony,' he murmured, his eyes lingering on her bare shoulders then trans- ferring to her naked mouth.

She sat up again and had to laugh. 'I must confess to feeling in rather remarkable spirits, although I probably look a fright.' She ran her hand through her hair again ruefully.

'No, you don't. You look good enough to tempt any man to tell the Cattlemen's Union to go back to their cows. But I'm glad you're in good spirits.' He handed her a glass of orange juice.

'I must be learning to be a m——' She stopped abruptly as their gazes caught and held, and his eyes sobered. She looked away and sipped the juice.

'Learning what?' he said very quietly.

She hesitated then grimaced. 'I wish I could unsay that—unfortunately it just slipped out.'

'Learning—to be a mistress, by any chance?' His hazel gaze was very direct.

She sighed. 'Something like that. I can't...I may not always be able to hide those...kinds of thoughts from you,' she said slowly. 'I guess that must have been buried away in my subconscious to—pop up like that. No.' She put the glass down, tucked the sheet more securely around her and drew up her knees. 'That's not true either; it's never really buried. But it wasn't *in* my mind when I said that. Because nothing can change the fact that up until a few moments ago I felt—wonderful, and it all had to do with being with you.' Her eyes were very blue and honest as she stared at him, then she felt the colour mounting in her face and she clasped her hands around her knees and laid her cheek on them. 'Have I ruined everything?'

He took so long to reply that she thought he wasn't going to, then she felt his hand on her hair and he said, 'It's difficult to ruin things for a man when you tell him he's made you feel wonderful. Should we concentrate on that?'

She lifted her head at last. 'Why not?' she murmured, and although her heart didn't feel so wonderful any longer she managed to smile wryly as she said again, 'Why not?'

It took her a while to get going after he left. She lay in a steaming bubble bath for some time, exploring her state of mind and trying to gauge Grant's. In one way, she had to admit, his admission and explanation last night was a relief. After he'd walked away from her on his last night at Heath House she'd thought he'd had total control. On the other hand, there was a wall beyond which he would not allow her to go—that was obvious. Any discussions, any lamentings on her part about the state of affairs between them he simply stonewalled, she thought glumly. And he didn't really give in without a fight last night, either, in a manner of speaking. Not that I meant to make a battle of it, but that's how it turned out for a while ...

She got out of the bath just before her skin started to wrinkle and dressed in a pair of baggy indigo jeans and a marvellous bomber jacket in a glowing pimento and embroidered with parachutes, slung a long scarf round her neck and set out to brave Melbourne's weather, which was as unpredictable as Tasmania's and decidedly grisly-looking.

She wasn't sure when the idea first crept into her mind but as the day wore on it became more and more deeply entrenched. Grant's last words to her had been, 'See you at four.' At three, she was ensconced in a cinema eating popcorn and drinking Coke, surrounded by packages and secure in the knowledge that she wouldn't be back at the hotel until five at least. A puny, perhaps petty kind of statement? she asked herself. Maybe, but one I need to make.

The film was actually engrossing but it was pouring when she came out, taxis were hard to come by and she arrived up at the suite at five-thirty, breathless and with raindrops netted in her hair, feeling guilty and flustered. Damn, she thought as she let herself in, dropped some parcels and tripped over them, what the hell am I coming to?

'Ah, Briony,' Grant said, 'I was beginning to wonder what had happened to you.'

She straightened, opened her mouth and saw that he was not alone. There was an extremely stylish woman of about thirty sitting at a paper-littered table with a briefcase open in front of her. So in the end all she said was a foolish, 'Oh!'

'Let me introduce you,' Grant murmured. 'This is Leonie Ledbetter, our in-house legal expert. Leonie, I'm sure you'll be interested to meet Briony Richards, the manager of Heath House and one of the chief architects of its success.'

Leonie Ledbetter rose with a charming smile and extended her hand. 'Indeed I would. How do you do? We're all most impressed with what Mr Goodman has told us of your operation.'

'How do you do?' Briony returned, a little feebly, she couldn't help thinking but the fact was she felt more than a little as if she'd just had the wind knocked out of her sails, and something else that was not nameable as yet but was surging up within her...

'Well, I'll be going, Mr Goodman!' Leonie turned back to the table and started to shovel papers into her briefcase. 'I'll fax the Wheeton agreement through to you for your signature tomorrow morning as soon as I've had it typed up. Please don't bother to see me out.' She crossed the room with another charming smile. 'I've wanted to see Cradle

Mountain for years, Miss Richards. In fact I'd love to do the Cradle Mountain-Lake St Clair walk—perhaps I'd be able to contact you for all the information one needs?'

'By all means,' Briony murmured. 'Perhaps Mr Goodman will bring you down on one of his visits?'

Leonie laughed and said ruefully, 'I'm hoping, I'm really hoping. Goodbye.' And she left.

Briony didn't actually see her go. She was staring at Grant with smouldering eyes. She also said after the door had closed and the suite lapsed into silence, 'Why don't you invite all your staff into our bedroom, Mr Goodman? I'm surprised that didn't occur to you!'

'Briony —— '

'Don't "Briony" me,' she returned furiously and flung her packages down on the floor. 'Or why not take out an ad in the *Melbourne Age*, the *Sydney Morning Herald*, the *Brisbane Courier Mail* so that the whole eastern seaboard of Australia is in *no* doubt at *all* that we're sleeping with each other?'

'Look, we knew we wouldn't be able to hide it,' he said coolly.

'We may not but that doesn't mean to say we have to *flaunt* it!'

'This was unexpected, Briony. Something came up, Leonie had to fly down from Sydney with some documents I had to see and we had to draft an agreement. And if,' he pointed out, 'you'd been five minutes later, you would have missed her.'

'What if I'd been here at four o'clock?' she demanded.

'Why weren't you here at four o'clock?' he asked drily.

'Because I decided to go to a movie! I decided,' she said scornfully, 'not to be waiting here for you like some—lap-dog, to be precise.'

'I can't imagine you being anyone's lap-dog, Briony,' he said with some irony. 'But if you had been here as we'd arranged you would have received the call I made to tell you this had come up out of the blue and that really the most practical place for Leonie and I to work things out was here, not only because I had some documents here *she* needed to see but because I had to make a number of interstate calls as well—and you would have had the option of—absenting yourself,' he said gently but there was nothing gentle about the rapier-like glint in his hazel eyes.

'Well, if you think that makes me feel guilty or stupid or whatever, it doesn't!' Briony said defiantly. 'Absenting myself, as you put it— how? Mooching around in the hotel bar or locking myself in the bedroom and afraid to make a sound? Neither of those appeals to me in the slightest, Grant,' she said grimly.

'Then had you thought of adopting purdah?' he queried mockingly. But as she picked up a packet of books off the floor and threw them at him he didn't even bother to dodge as they went wide and he advanced on her menacingly. 'No, enough, Briony.' His fingers closed round her wrists like bands of steel. 'You're being ridiculous.' He stared down into her stormy eyes then fleetingly down at her heaving breasts. 'All you had to do was conduct yourself with composure and grace——'

'I don't feel composed and I don't feel in a state of grace!'

He released her wrists and she rocked on her heels. 'Then maybe we ought to call the whole thing off,' he said evenly.

She went to hit him and ended up in his arms. 'That doesn't go down well either?' he drawled. 'Perhaps you better tell me *your* solution because I'm running out of ideas, but, in the meantime, in case this is a farewell...' He shrugged and drew her closer.

'Don't!' she warned furiously. 'To kiss me now would be the height of hackney ——'

'It might be,' he agreed. 'You know I thought there was more between us but it seems I was wrong. Is all this to force a wedding-ring out of me, Briony? Now how hackneyed would that be?' he marvelled, and stilled the convulsive movement she made with easy strength. 'I wouldn't fight this,' he added barely audibly. 'We both know that in spite of all sorts of differences we are united in one thing at least. We want each other quite desperately at times—not to put too fine a point on it.' And he started to kiss her.

Ten hectic, passionate minutes later he'd removed her colourful jacket and removed *her* to the settee, where she lay in his lap with her head on his shoulder and the knowledge in her heart that he was right. Because even in anger and a growing sense of despair, even as she'd fought him virtually tooth and nail, the sheer explosiveness of their need for each other had gradually taken over. It was as if the hostility between them had fuelled their desire to greater heights. But it was impossible to maintain that hostility when your senses were quivering, your whole being was concentrated upon a man as if he was your lifeline and the prospect of being without him to nourish your soul and your body was terrifying.

When she did speak at last it was to say the first thing that came to mind. 'This has never happened to me before...'

He fingered the sleeve of her green T-shirt. 'Hasn't it?'

She winced. 'You may find that hard to believe but it's true.'

'When you say "this", what do you mean exactly?' He stilled her protesting movement and ran his fingers through her hair gently. 'I'm not being deliberately obtuse or gratuitously curious,' he added. 'But it would be interesting to try and work out why we do affect each other so—intensely.' His fingers wandered down to her chin and he tilted it so that she was forced to look into his eyes.

Briony ran her tongue over her bruised lips. 'How can I answer that when it—when I *haven't* felt this way before?' she said huskily. 'Have you?'

'Not—for a long time.'

'Not...since Lisa?'

His lips twisted. 'I've always refrained from making those kind of comparisons.'

'Isn't that what you're asking me to do, though?'

He smiled slightly and wound a curl of her hair round his finger. 'I think what I'm trying to do is find a way for us to go on in a kind of peace. Briony, why does the thought of people knowing about us upset you so much? And, before you say anything, I understood about Heath House.'

She was silent for a long time as it occurred to her that that wasn't really the problem— not what other people thought but what she thought of herself. It was that making her so unsettled and ready to turn into a virago; it was the thought that this relationship held little hope for her of permanence, complete fulfilment, and that he was steadfastly never failing to make her aware of it. But if she felt as she had moments ago about losing Grant how would she feel as she fell more and more in love with him?

'Briony?'

'Grant——' she swallowed '——you once cherished the thought that I tried to break up Nick Semple's marriage.'

'You didn't deny it,' he said sombrely.

'I know,' she said carefully. 'But I don't think you're the kind of person who would sleep with me unless you'd...not exactly forgiven me but squared it with your conscience somehow, yet it still has to be at the back of your mind.'

'I suppose so.'

'Well, how have you dealt with it?' she asked, her eyes suddenly very blue and very direct.

'How have I dealt with it?' He laid his head back and grimaced. 'We all make mistakes but you at least had the gallantry to admit yours and cop the fallout, that's how, I guess. If there's one thing—no, among some things I'm unsure of, one of them is how you really felt about Nick, though. And I suppose it would be true to say that I was unable to suppress the very base desire to—obliterate him from your memory.'

Briony gasped.

'That upsets you?'

'No...yes...there was no reason...' She stopped abruptly then whispered intensely, '*Why*?'

He lifted his head and stared down at her soberly. 'Men are like that, unfortunately. But what I found was not quite what I expected. You may—you do exhibit some worldliness, Briony. You're touchy, you fought me every inch of the way, you're obviously cynical and you appear to have had certain ambitions regarding Nick, but you make love to me...differently. Almost as if there hasn't been anyone in your life for a long time.'

She opened her mouth, closed it and could only stare mutely into his eyes.

'So,' he said very quietly, 'if I baffle you at times, the feeling is mutual.' And he laid his palm on her cheek.

Briony licked her lips. 'You accused me of trying to force a wedding-ring out of you not very long ago. Do you really believe that, Grant? Do you still believe I'm on that same old track, in other words?'

He answered obliquely. 'What would make you happy, Briony? Happy in bed and out of it, with me?'

She closed her eyes and said starkly, 'I don't know. Some people are destined to—be that way, aren't they?'

'We've not given ourselves much chance to prove or disprove that. Look, I'm sorry about Leonie.' He traced the outline of her mouth gently. 'And for what it's worth I'd love to transport you to some uninhabited South Sea island but we do have three more days together and, to the best of my knowledge, alone.'

Her lashes lifted and her heart jolted at the way he was looking down at her and she was assailed by desire. 'I...I don't know how we...didn't end up in bed a little while ago,' she said helplessly.

'There's always now.'

There was.

'You shouldn't be doing this like this,' she said, however, as he set her on the bedroom floor and pulled her T-shirt free of her jeans.

'Undressing you?' His hazel eyes glinted wryly.

'I meant—what I meant was...I think I meant I wish to God I could be as contained as you are sometimes right now,' she said frustratedly as her bare skin shivered beneath his fingers and her bra fell to the floor.

'What makes you think I'm contained?' he queried and stared down at her breasts.

'You just seem to be, that's all,' she replied unevenly, and suddenly hugged herself almost defensively.

'Tell you what, were you to undress me you'd find out how supremely wrong you are.'

'Oh,' she said disconcertedly, her arms falling to her sides, which he took advantage of to cup her breasts and stroke her nipples into aching peaks.

'Mmm...quite wrong. Try it.'

Her lips quivered then she was laughing softly as she unbuttoned his shirt and slipped her hands beneath it. 'I don't know what's wrong with me. I feel as if I'm on a see-saw.' She ran her hands up and down his back and he held her into his body. 'Mmm,' she murmured. 'I see what you mean.'

'That's not quite true,' he said gravely.

'And that's splitting hairs,' she reprimanded him, but still smiling, and she disengaged herself. 'I think we should—well, since we're going to do this——'

'You think we should get on with it?'

'Something like that,' she agreed.

'Thank God,' he replied fervently and proceeded to complete her undressing swiftly. 'I was a doomed man otherwise.'

Some time later he sat up beside her and swore.

'What?' Briony asked anxiously, sitting up too.

'I forgot. I've got tickets for *The Phantom of the Opera* tonight. Have you seen it?'

'No! Oh...'

'Would you like to?'

'I'd *love* to, but——'

'But what?'

'You didn't sound too enthusiastic a moment ago.'

'I had other things on my mind,' he said gravely. 'From which I didn't at the time, welcome being distracted.'

'Such as?' she queried innocently.

'You,' he replied promptly and, taking her in his arms, lay back with her. 'You were wonderful,' he said in a different voice.

'So were you.' She smoothed her palm along his shoulder and marvelled at how calm and warm and wonderful she felt when an hour or so ago she'd been throwing books around. She winced.

'What?'

'Nothing—well, I feel like a different person, that's all.'

He smiled and kissed her lightly. 'How long will it take you to get ready?'

'Depends on how much I have to dress up.'

'I've booked a box—you did say something about a dress that was strapless and backless.'

'Ah. I exaggerated slightly. It's strapless but not exactly backless.'

'Nevertheless this might be good time to wear it.'

'Why is that?'

'Because, my enchanting witch ——' he stared down into her mischievous eyes '—having just made love to you, I might be able to control myself for a while.'

She chuckled. 'Well, I better get ready.'

But he joined her in the shower.

'Is this a good idea?' she gasped as he slid the glass door aside and watched the water slipping down her body.

He stepped in. 'I don't know. It was something I couldn't resist.' He touched her breasts lightly. 'They're perfect—did you know?'

'Well, I—not perfect, surely?'

'Perfect,' he said gravely. 'I have watched them beneath an assortment of shirts, dresses and the like, I have had them on my mind in some really improbable places such as the peak of Cradle Mountain, in some impossible situations where I could have got myself a black eye had I made the slightest allusion to my growing fascination with them—not to mention the rest of you.' And he slid his hands down her waist. 'You're beautiful, Briony. Would you like to know what one of my first fantasies was?'

Her lips parted as his hands wandered over the paler skin of her upper thighs, her hips and waist.

'I'll tell you anyway. In the Ballroom Forest that day you led Dwight and Dora and Co. there, and the only times you looked at me if looks could kill I should have died on the spot several times over. I had this fantasy then of just the two of us being there, perhaps hot and dusty, perhaps—taking off our clothes and refreshing ourselves in the stream. I visualised the dappled sunlight playing over your skin, the water streaming off your breasts, how your body would glisten and be—a delight to behold.'

Briony took a ragged breath but then her lips started to curve into a wry smile.

'I know,' he said, smiling ruefully himself. 'Once I felt the water it occurred to me it would put a dampener on the most ardent— ambitions. We would have frozen,' he said simply.

She laughed outright.

'I'm only telling you this,' he said, resuming a serious expression, 'so you will know that in some respects, concerning you, notably, I'm not as contained as you seem to think.'

She grimaced then said softly, 'Thanks.' And she slipped her arms round his neck, pressed her wet breasts against him. 'Thanks.'

The dress was the same blue as her eyes and it hugged her breasts, fitted her waist then billowed out to her feet. With it she had a quilted silver jacket and silver shoes.

But if his expression told her she looked stunning he all but took her breath away in a beautifully tailored black dinner-suit that emphasised his height and the width of his shoulders.

'Wow!' she said huskily. 'You look super!'

'So do you—let's get out of here,' he said with a thoroughly wicked little glint in his eye.

They did more—they went on to supper after *The Phantom* at a club with a band and danced the rest of the night away. They got back to the hotel at four-thirty laughing at the time, and he took her beautiful dress off her and carried her to bed like a child.

'Mmm...' she said sleepily as he lay down beside her some minutes later. 'Thank you for a wonderful evening...'

'My pleasure,' he murmured and drew her into his arms.

She relaxed against him and felt her mind fall away towards sleep but she said, because the curious thought was in her mind, 'I'm so glad you're not a phantom.'

'No—sweet dreams, Briony.'

But by then she was asleep and she missed the way he watched her with oddly bleak eyes for a time.

CHAPTER EIGHT

THEY slept until late morning then had a lazy breakfast in bed. The weather was wet and cold so Briony closed the curtains against it and returned to bed.

'Such sloth,' she remarked to Grant, who was sitting back reading the paper.

'What did you have in mind?'

She stretched and yawned. 'Going back to sleep,' she said with a grin.

In fact they spent the whole day in the suite as the weather got worse, and it was a day to cherish, she thought once. They talked, watched a video or were just quiet together as the mood took them. She showed him all her purchases and he sent out for a compact disc of *The Phantom of the Opera* and other Andrew Lloyd Webber music to add to her collection. She told him about her mother, who seemed at last to have found a man to replace her father, and her sister who was two years younger but already married with three children.

'Not another managerial whiz in the making?' he queried.

'No.' Briony grimaced. 'She started out studying law then love hit her on the head— but she seems to be very happy.'

'Don't they miss you?'

'I . . . I suppose so,' Briony said slowly.

'Since you're over here, why don't you go and see them? I'm sure Linda can cope without you for another couple of days.'

She smiled. 'Perhaps I will. Talking of Linda, I—— '

'No, let's not,' he said wryly. 'I'm sure if any disaster has befallen Heath House we'd have heard by now. Come here.' He held out his hand.

She came and curled up in his lap. All she wore was a thigh-length cotton shirt and a pair of panties. All he wore was a pair of jeans. 'What should we do this evening?' he asked. 'Since we've spent such a slothful day.'

'I don't mind, and I've enjoyed every minute of it. I didn't imagine you could— well, relax like this.'

He looked down at her with a crooked smile. 'It wouldn't have been nearly so easy without you. As a matter of fact, in view of

your expertise and endurance where mountains are concerned, not to mention the way
you run an hotel, I was surprised you didn't
want to be doing something wildly energetic.'

She laughed and snuggled closer. 'Then
we've surprised each other. Mind you,
we've...climbed a few mountains together
in...other respects.'

'So we have. But not for nearly twenty-four
hours,' he said gravely.

'Well, no.'

'So, I had this thought.' His hands slid
under her shirt. 'Supposing we took ourselves
back to bed for an interlude——how would you
then feel about going out to a little, not smart,
Italian restaurant I know where they make a
wonderful, hearty minestrone, where their
scallopini alla whatever you like is renowned,
or their pasta, again however you like, is
superb and their lasagne——'

'Stop!' she begged. 'My mouth's watering!
Should we wait?'

'Oh, definitely.' His thumbs moved on her
nipples and she drew a sudden breath. 'A
much better idea than having to dash back
here and leave our meal half-finished. I've

decided that has to be my strategy from now on.'

'You're teasing me, Grant Goodman,' she said gravely and traced the lines beside his mouth.

He grimaced. 'I'm not, you know.' And he withdrew his hands but only to unbutton her shirt and lay it aside. Briony didn't have to glance down to know that her nipples were standing erect from his touch but she gasped as he moved her slightly and bent his head so he could take one throbbing peak gently between his teeth.

'Oh...' It was a bare breath of sound and her head fell back over his arm; she raised one hand distractedly to press her fingers through his hair then down his neck and across his shoulders with growing urgency. And just when she thought she couldn't take any more, as wave after exquisite wave of feeling washed over her, he transferred his lips to hers. But his hand sought her panties and he slipped them lower and lower and as his fingers roamed softly through the springy curls at the base of her stomach she was immediately on another rollercoaster.

'Grant, no...it's too much,' she said huskily, but it wasn't. Because if she thought she'd desired Grant Goodman before she was in more desperate need of him now than ever.

'Too much?' he said very quietly between kissing her throat. 'I wonder if we'll ever get enough of each other, Briony...?'

She wore her bomber jacket with the parachutes and jeans to his Italian restaurant and he wore jeans and a brightly patterned pullover. She was quiet and so was he, yet he held her close in the taxi and kept her close beside him as they ate.

It occurred to her to ask him about what he'd said but she discarded the idea because she didn't have the strength of mind, she found. It was as if she was cocooned against everything but their last lovemaking and it was a strange sensation for her, she realised. It was a sort of utter dependence on Grant at the moment...

When they'd finished their coffee he said, 'We have a choice. We can call a cab or we could walk. It's only about half an hour and I think it's cleared up.'

'Let's walk.' She smiled at him.

The night was bright and sparkling as they left, with neon lights reflecting in the puddles on the pavement and stars overhead. It was also cool and they walked briskly, hand in hand, savouring the clean, salty tang in the air. They only stopped once and that was to look into a pet shop window.

'Oh, no,' Briony said softly, 'it shouldn't be allowed.'

'You like dogs?'

'I love them.' The black and white puppy in the window sat up and yawned and wagged its tail hopefully. 'I wonder what he is?'

'A mixture, I should say,' Grant said wryly.

Briony smiled. 'Goodnight, baby,' she said gently and turned away.

Grant glanced at her thoughtfully. 'I don't suppose it would be very practical to have one at Heath House.'

'It would probably be the last place.' Briony grimaced. 'What with guests, wombats, possums and the like.'

He took her hand and grinned. 'You make them all sound like the one species—guests, wombats and possums. But I suppose you could train a dog—we turn left here.'

'I'm glad you thought of walking,' she said, unwinding her scarf back in the suite. 'All that marvellous food——' She stopped as the phone buzzed discreetly.

Grant answered and she watched his face sober. Then he said curtly into the phone, 'Well, what do *you* think it is?'

'What?' she said anxiously as he put the phone down a few moments later.

'It's Hannah. A really high temperature, swollen glands—possibly glandular fever but they can't be sure yet. Briony——'

'Are you going to ask me if I understand? Of *course* I do. You get on to the airlines and I'll start packing for you.'

He closed his eyes briefly then took her in his arms. 'I'm sorry,' he said very quietly. 'Things—aren't going our way at all, are they? I wanted to give you something——'

'Grant——' her eyes were very blue and direct '—if you think I need gifts then you don't know me at all.'

'I——' He stopped and appeared to change tack. 'What will you do?'

She grimaced. 'Go back to work probably—no——' she touched his face with her fingertips '—I've had a wonderful time.

Thank you. And don't worry about me, I'll
be fine.'

Famous last words, she thought, when she
was alone in the suite an hour later. I wonder
if I'll ever be the same again?

She wandered into the bedroom and stared
at her two new dresses in the wardrobe, the
black one and the blue, and then to still the
growing storm of emotion in her heart she
came to a sudden decision. She would pay her
mother and her sister a flying visit.

It was strange being in Sydney, knowing Grant
was in the same city, and she was tempted to
ring him to ask about Hannah. But a glance
through the telephone directory revealed no
G. Goodmans in any likely suburb and the
thought of doing it through his office did not
appeal to her.

So she spent the day with her mother and
her sister Sarah, reacquainted herself with her
nieces and nephew and spent the night with
her mother, which included a heart-to-heart
chat that began thus . . .

'I'm so glad to see you, darling. I rather
got the feeling you had decided to abandon
us as well.' Serena Richards looked at Briony

thoughtfully as they shared a nightcap in her small but pretty flat. 'In fact,' she continued, 'I'd made up my mind to come to the wilds of Tasmania very shortly.'

'I wasn't—of course I didn't mean to abandon you,' Briony protested. 'Look how often I write and ring you.'

'I know.' Her mother smiled. 'I've kept every letter, not only for sentimental reasons but because it's been a charming commentary on the joys and disasters of running a hotel but... Briony, you wouldn't tell me why you left Sydney so suddenly. I could only presume it was an unhappy love-affair.'

'What made you assume that?'

'Well, I know you well enough to know you wouldn't have been pinching or pilfering, darling,' her mother said with gentle reproach. 'I also know you well enough to know how ambitious you are—or were.'

Briony grimaced then she sighed abruptly. 'Something like that. Mum, from *your* letters, I get the feeling you might even be thinking of getting married again. And you look— wonderful,' she said with genuine admiration.

Serena Richards coloured faintly and said, 'Would you mind?'

'Mind! Why should I? I'd only love you to be happy.'

'I've got the feeling there's some role-reversal going on here,' Serena said ruefully, then she sobered. 'There is one thing I wanted to say to you, though, Briony. I know how hard it is to talk about these things, even to a mother, or perhaps especially to a mother, but—well, I'm always here to confide in and I might even be able to help. You see,' she went on slowly as if choosing her words with care, 'I often worried that... love might be a problem for you.'

Briony blinked. 'Why?' she whispered.

'You're so attractive for one thing——'

'No more than Sarah.'

'No. But there's a different quality to it and Sarah has a much more easygoing nature. I think falling in love for her was a——' Serena gestured '——comfortable, happy process. But for you—well, I was always a little afraid it... wouldn't *be* like that for you.'

'Why?' Briony said again, staring at her mother out of slightly stunned eyes.

'Darling, don't look like that,' Serena said gently. 'I always knew men would tend to make fools of themselves over you; you're not only attractive but so...vital. And ever since you were about two and refused to cry whenever I had to point out the error of your ways to you but looked me up and down with incredible hauteur, when you were not much older and persuading you not to do things you'd set your heart on required the wisdom of Solomon, I knew—certain things would not be easy for you.'

'They—aren't,' Briony said starkly. 'But if only you knew—well...' She stopped and shrugged.

'Tell me, my dear.'

Briony stood up and walked across the room. 'There've only been two men of any consequence,' she said abruptly, 'although I had thought I was in love a couple of times before that. But the first of these two was a liar and a cheat—and I wasn't even in love with him, while the second... The second,' she said with a slight break in her voice, 'is the one man I can't seem to stay away from, but I doubt I'll ever be more to him than— an unwilling mistress, and when I say that you probably can't begin to guess the awful irony of it.'

'My dear, no man is worth that,' Serena said quietly.

'Do you think I haven't told myself that?'

'Then keep telling yourself—look, it's easy for me to say, I know, but things change, Briony. You may even look back on this man one day and wonder what you saw in him . . .'

She flew to Launceston the next morning and drove back to Heath House, and all the way she couldn't get her mother's words out of her mind—'. . . no man is worth that.'

'Briony!' Linda said as she walked into the reception office. 'Welcome back, and am I glad to see you!'

'Hi, Linda. And thanks—but what's gone wrong?'

'Nothing's *wrong*,' Linda said hastily, 'but this arrived half an hour ago and it's for you. Here's the letter that came with it.' She thrust an envelope into Briony's hand. 'Damn,' she added as the bell on the front desk rang, 'it's behind the desk.'

Briony frowned and tore open the envelope and read the typed note.

I've had him checked out and he's as sound as a bell plus he's had all his shots.

I leave the problem of guests, wombats and possums up to you... Missing you, Grant. P.S. Hannah is recovering well.

Briony lifted her head, her eyes widening and her mouth falling open. It was only a few steps to the desk and behind it was a basket with a black and white puppy curled up in it. She closed her eyes then sank down on to her knees. The puppy pricked its ears then sat up and gazed at her soulfully. She put out a hand and stroked him gently whereupon his whole small body started to shudder in ecstasy and he licked her hand adoringly. She picked him up and hugged him and found herself thinking that she would always know what she saw in Grant Goodman, that was the problem...

'But,' Linda said, 'it's not going to be easy. Where will you keep him to start with?'

'In my suite. But he can sleep on my service porch.'

'Have you any idea how destructive puppies can be, not to mention messy?'

'Yes. I'll just have to train him.'

'Rather you than me. What will you call him?'

'I don't know—yes, I do, I'll call him Oliver because I think he's been rather like a little lost boy up until now.'

Linda stared down at the dog somewhat bemusedly. 'Well—how was your holiday?'

'Lovely, thanks. Anything I should know about?'

Linda shook herself out of her bemused state. 'Briony,' she said proudly, 'I hesitate to say I coped as well as you do but I coped pretty damn well all the same!'

It was a month before she saw Grant again. Then he rang her from the seaside town of Strahan, about an hour from Cradle Mountain, and suggested she drive down to meet him.

A clamour of emotions rose within Briony. She'd spoken to him often over the past weeks, some of them long, leisurely calls, and in a sense although she'd missed him almost unbearably at times she'd felt oddly un-pressured. Yet, she'd acknowledged, that was only because without his presence she'd pushed all the problems of their relationship to the back of her mind. Now they all came to the fore at once...

'Briony?' he said down the line.

'Yes, I'm still here.' She bit her lip.

'Will you come? We could spend two nights here and then a couple at Heath House. I want to see how the new buildings are going.'

'I—yes.' She closed her eyes and her shoulders sagged in something like defeat.

Franklin Manor, built in 1890 and totally refurbished in 1988, was a superb example of Tasmanian colonial accommodation yet with all the discreet modern-day luxuries, and in any other circumstances Briony would have been vitally interested in this 'property', as they said in the trade. As it was, as she pulled her car into a car park and saw Grant strolling out to meet her, the beautiful old mansion and just about all else faded from her mind.

But she didn't say much until they were up in the room he'd booked. Even then she was constrained and awkward and she fiddled with her bag, looking around for somewhere to put it, before she pulled off her coat and went to hang it up, then busied herself with her cosmetic case.

He stood and watched her narrowly with his hands shoved into his pockets for a moment, then he said gently, 'How's Oliver?'

'Fine!' she said brightly. 'You'd be amazed how he's grown and how intelligent he is. He's even beginning to understand about possums and wombats and how they're off limits.'

'Who's looking after him?'

'Linda. She's become a devotee.' She grimaced and stopped at last, her hands empty, her eyes shadowed and wary. And they stared at each other for an age. He was casually dressed in khaki trousers and a green and white checked shirt with the sleeves rolled up to below his elbows. His tawny hair was wind-blown, as if he'd been out walking, and every line and angle of his face, every plane of his tall, strong body seemed to imprint itself on her heart.

'It's been too long, hasn't it?' he said soberly at last. 'I'm sorry.'

She shrugged slightly. 'I guess it can't be helped.'

'I didn't realise—from the way we spoke on the phone these past weeks—that you felt like this.'

'I didn't.' She hesitated. 'It just seems to have hit me now, whatever it is.' She tried to smile. 'Well, from when you rang. And I'm not quite sure what it is...'

He didn't say anything for a moment then he held out his hand.

Briony blinked away sudden tears and put hers into it. Then she went slowly into his arms and he simply held her for a long time, massaging the back of her neck as she laid her cheek against his shoulder.

It worked after a time. 'Sorry,' she said wryly but making no attempt to move. 'I don't know what got into me.'

'Briony ── '

'No, Grant,' she broke in with sudden resolution. 'I really didn't come to Strahan to...make a fuss. Well...' She lifted her gaze to his at last and said softly, 'You've got me for two days. What shall we do?'

'Briony...' His hazel eyes were sombre but she put a finger to his lips.

'Believe it or not I've never been to the Gateway to the World heritage area, I've only glimpsed Macquarie Harbour so far, I've never seen the Gordon river and the ancient rainforests that line its banks, or Sarah Island or Huon pines growing, or Ocean Beach and the twenty-thousand-kilometre expanse of sea that separates it from South America and the swells ripped up by the ''roaring forties'' and the muttonbird rookeries—' She stopped as a smile started to grow at the back of his eyes.

'You've certainly done your homework.'

She relaxed. 'All learnt from a pamphlet, sir. I can't tell you how many people I've sent to Strahan and how many times I've promised myself I should at least see the place before I send any more!'

'Well, I would love to show you Strahan but may I at least kiss you first?'

Her mouth dimpled at the corners. 'I was beginning to think you'd never ask.'

They had dinner that night at the Pub Café on the waterfront, part of Hamer's Hotel, also refurbished.

'The place is booming!' Briony said as she tucked into a delicious lobster.

'As you detailed so well earlier,' Grant commented, 'there are a lot of remarkable things to see and do in the area and a lot of history, convict and otherwise. I suppose, too, the Franklin below Gordon river system is one of the last great wildernesses.'

'And it's really only a village—I love it!' She gazed out of the window across the road to the colourful waterfront, where a couple of cruise boats were tied up, a yacht, two fishing boats, their decks piled high with wicker lobster pots, and a seaplane bobbing gently on the waters of Macquarie Harbour.

'Its tourist potential seems undoubted.'

Briony looked across at him, suddenly alerted. 'Are you—is that why you're here?' she queried.

'I'm looking at a property, yes.'

'I might have known,' she said wryly.

'You don't think it would be a good idea to have two Tasmanian properties?'

'I think the way you do things it's probably a very good idea. I think, from the look of the visitors streaming in here, you're right about the potential. I think the possibilities of a "package" between a property here and Heath House would be well worth exploring. For people driving from Hobart I should imagine the well-worn route would be Strahan— and of course there's Queenstown on the way—Cradle Mountain. From Launceston it's invariably Strahan after Cradle Mountain.'

'You've read my mind, Briony,' he murmured, and raised his wine glass to her. But then he changed the subject completely, or so she thought. 'Would you like to fly over the Gordon river tomorrow morning? They say it's quite a sight.'

'I'd love to.' She sat back with a sigh. 'You're going to have to walk me again, Grant.'

He smiled at her. 'A pleasure. But I have other plans for you as well.'

'Oh?'

'Mmm. I'll tell you when the time comes.'

'Once again, I might have known.'

'I always promised myself this but we never quite got round to it.'

Briony spread her arms out and laid her head back. The spa bubbled around them and their legs were entwined. Her hair was damp with the steam and curling madly and her skin above the water was pink and glistening.

'What are you thinking?' he asked.

'I'm not. I decided . . .' she paused and sat up a bit ' . . . not to think too much today.'

'And tomorrow?'

'The same. There's one problem about these spas, Grant. Your skin can go crinkly if you stay in them too long.'

'So?'

'I think I might be in the pre-crinkly stage!' And with a swift, lithe movement she pulled herself out. But he put a restraining hand around her ankle. 'Grant,' she protested.

'I only mean—wait for me,' he said mildly and released her ankle to come out himself. 'I very much like handling your body when it's wet, you see,' he said gravely, and proceeded to do just that.

'Oh, dear.' She sighed and put her hands on his shoulders.

He laughed down at her. 'Anyone would think you were an old married lady,' he teased.

'Old!'

'I meant, of course, in terms of having to humour a husband.' The lines beside his mouth were a give-away although he spoke seriously.

'Well, I doubt if I'll ever be that,' she answered in the same vein, and then it hit her—what he'd said and what she'd said—

and she went still beneath his hands, her eyes widened and then she closed them in pain.

'Briony —— '

'No, Grant,' she whispered, and freed herself. 'Don't say anything.' She reached for a towelling robe and wrapped herself in it and wound a towel round her hair turban-wise. 'I wouldn't mind a cup of coffee. How about you?' She didn't wait for an answer.

'We obviously have to talk about this, Briony,' he said about ten minutes later when the air was filled with the aroma of coffee and he'd pulled on a tracksuit. She still wore her robe but she'd taken the towel off her hair and was sitting curled up on the bed with her coffee.

'I don't think we should do anything *obvious* at all, Grant,' she replied evenly. 'I'm only sorry I was so thin-skinned—I didn't mean to be, believe me.' She shrugged and ran her fingers through her hair then looked up tensely as he came to stand beside the bed. 'I know what you're going to say anyway. Lovers and friends, that's how it has to be. I just wish to God you weren't also my *boss*,' she finished intensely.

'I don't think that makes as much difference as you seem to imagine.'

'I know—you've never thought that. Oh, God,' she whispered, and put the back of her hand to her mouth. 'Have you any idea how humiliating it is to be going through this routine, Grant? For the life of me I just wish I could play this game the way you want it; I'd love to give you a real run for your money instead of this,' she said starkly. 'But I don't seem to be made that way.'

'A run for my money?' he said slowly. 'Is that what you think I'm doing to you, Briony?'

'I don't...no, I don't,' she said tiredly, then made another effort. 'But, while you can obviously be happy to have me as a very small part of your life, I—can't be that way. I think I must be one of those ''all or nothing'' people. My mother certainly tried to tell me I was—or something to that effect.'

He was silent for a long time. Then he said, 'Do you know what being married to me would be like? Not a lot different from what we have now. But you wouldn't have the compensations you have now, the freedom——'

'*Why*?' she said on a sobbing little breath.

He stood up and went over to the window, pushing the curtains aside. 'It's the way I'm made, probably,' he said drily at last. 'For one thing I'm a workaholic—you may not know this but I wasn't born with a silver spoon in my mouth. I wrestled one cattle property through years of one disaster after another from the time I was about seventeen before it came good and I could branch out. And it's a residue from Lisa, no doubt. Look, let's be honest. We're two complicated people. We *both*, I think, have sides to us that are tough, cynical and ambitious.

'You . . .' he paused and turned suddenly to look at her ' . . . told me that you'd made one mistake in your life. Believe me, I've done some things I regret too, and there are at least two women I've hurt—unforgivably because I failed to make them understand how I am. But at least, Briony, *you* must know what it's like to be this way.'

She stared at him with her lips parted.

'And if we were ever to get to the stage of trying to change each other, which we no doubt would in a marriage—I often think that's why so many marriages fail—we could create our own little hell.'

'Is that how you see me?' she said huskily after a strained, incredulous pause.

'My dear,' he said sombrely, 'you're only twenty-seven but your strength of purpose, your skills in this business are as good if not better than anyone else I've come across. And you must know the kind of toughness et cetera, that requires.'

She licked her lips. 'I thought I did,' she said barely audibly and stared down at her coffee-cup. Then she raised her blue eyes to his. 'Grant, you indicated once you didn't like Nick Semple a lot. Is...he still...in your business?'

He looked at her narrowly. 'Just,' he said grimly. 'Angelique is pregnant. Why do you ask?'

She looked away and took a breath. 'I...it doesn't matter.'

'Believe me, Briony, it's a long time since I believed Nick was as pure and lily-white in regard to you as the Semples made out. Do you want to go through it all blow-by-blow? We can if you like, but to be honest again...' he paused and that steady hazel gaze seemed to look right through to her soul '...if there's any guilt in your heart, it's probably better left unsaid. I think you've made your reparations, and to me that's all that matters.'

Any guilt in my heart? Briony thought, and winced. 'All right.'

'Does that mean you think we can—go on?'

'I . . .' She put a hand to her eyes.

'So far as this business of being your boss goes,' he said quietly, 'I would like to make things more equitable between us, Briony, and this is what I had in mind. My mainland Australian operations are all in partnership with the Semple family—as you know. But when I bought Heath House I set up a separate company so they have no part in it. But I'd like to offer *you* a share in this new company that will operate Heath House and this property I plan to buy in Strahan.'

Briony gasped and her cup rocked in her hands. He took it from her, put it down and sat down beside her. 'That would make us more like partners and no longer just boss and employee. Nor would it be anything but good business sense if that should bother you. I need your dedication and expertise. And there is no better or fairer way to pay for those things than to cut someone in.'

'I don't believe it,' she whispered.

'Why not? You would find it's a practice I often follow if you went back through my businesses. And I've had this at the back of my mind for a while, which is why the original contract I talked about offering you never materialised.'

She closed her eyes briefly because she'd wondered about the contract that had never materialised although her salary had increased as he'd promised. Wondered and hoped against hope that there were other reasons for it to have been abandoned, if it had. That hope now died. 'What if we ... fell out?' she said with an effort.

'That's hard to visualise,' he said quietly, and picked up her hand. He stared down at it in his for a long moment then looked up into her eyes, and she trembled at what she saw in his. He waited briefly then went on, 'Perhaps this is what I should have said first of all. I want you and need you, Briony, to the exclusion of all else. I couldn't share you with anyone and you wouldn't be sharing me with anyone.'

For some reason this made her smile.

'Do you doubt it?'

'No... Well, no.' Her smile faded. 'Grant, I can't make up my mind here and now. No,' she said as he went to speak. 'A lot of what you've said is probably true but I think I have to look into my heart and try to see what's really there. And in the meantime could we go on being just lovers and friends for a little longer?'

He didn't answer but put his arms around her and pulled her back so that they were both lying half on the bed, and he ran his fingers through her damp, springy hair then opened her robe and did the same to her still, pink, satiny body.

CHAPTER NINE

IT WAS a busy day the next day. They made the seaplane trip over the famed south-western corner of Tasmania, which gave them a bird's-eye view of the Franklin and Gordon rivers, then they landed at St John Falls in a beautiful amphitheatre of rainforest on the mirror-like surface of the Gordon. But what was quite stunning was the absolute silence once the plane's engine died—and then the sound of birds and waterfalls.

Briony thought Grant was unusually silent as they stood on the pontoon listening, silent and oddly withdrawn as he stared around with his back to her, yet he hadn't been earlier despite her refusal to give him an answer to his proposition. In fact, on waking, he'd made lovely, gentle love to her and made her feel different—cherished was the word, she thought, as she watched him and wondered at his mood now in this beautiful, special place. It was almost as if it was a revelation to him, but what kind of revelation she had no idea.

Then it occurred to her that she should be seeking revelations of her own, but it seemed impossible to look beyond the fact that she either accepted what he'd offered, or she gave up Grant Goodman and accepted a life of loneliness and pain. Was the acid test which would bring the greater pain? *Had* he read her accurately, more accurately than she knew herself? Would it make any difference if she told him the truth about Nick Semple...?

They had a look at his proposed purchase after lunch, a run-down guest house but on a site with wonderful views, and when she asked him if he planned to pull it down and rebuild he didn't answer. He seemed to be lost in thought again. So much so that when they got back to Franklin Manor and were getting ready for dinner she asked him if anything was wrong.

He looked up. 'No. Why?' He had his trousers on and a shirt, but unbuttoned as yet, and his hair was hanging in his eyes.

She was trying to do up the zip of her dress, the red dress she'd worn the first night they'd laid eyes on each other, and he came up behind her and did it for her. 'Thanks.' She was facing a mirror and he stood behind her, staring absently down at the back of her neck. Briony frowned. 'I just wondered,' she murmured, and went to move away, but he put his hands on her waist and raised his eyes to hers in the mirror.

'I remember this dress,' he said lightly.

'Do you?'

'Yes. I also remember thinking how well it became you—in fact how well anything would become you.'

Briony hesitated then leant back against him. 'You managed to transmit those sentiments,' she said wryly. 'I felt as if I'd put it on specially *for* you——'

'Which annoyed you considerably?'

'Which annoyed me considerably,' she agreed.

His lips twisted. 'We've had our moments, haven't we?'

'Are they—about to end?' she asked huskily.

His hands moved rather abruptly then he smoothed the red material over her hips. 'Why do you ask that?'

She turned to face him slowly. 'There's something on your mind. I saw it happen earlier today when we were on the Gordon River... Is it because I haven't said yes immediately?' Her eyes were direct but wary.

He took his time answering but then he said only, 'How long do you think it will take you to look into your heart, Briony?'

Her lips parted. 'I didn't realise there was a time limit.'

'There's not, as such. But I don't suppose it would help either of us to drag it out.'

'Grant—this is my life you're talking about,' she whispered.

'I know. Have you stopped to think of your life—without this?' His hands opened out over her back and he drew her closer so that their bodies were touching.

'That's... this really is blackmail...'

'No,' he said quietly. 'It's facing reality. It's asking yourself whether another man can do the things I do to you, can make you feel the way I do.'

She stared up at him and it struck her that there were two sides to Grant Goodman; the one she loved, the one that appealed not only to the sensuous side of her but made any day a better day just to be in his company—and a side to him that was as immutable as the face of Cradle Mountain... And it was that side she was facing now because she couldn't read his expression other than to know that if she'd thought herself under siege before it was nothing to now. And it occurred to her that there was only one weapon left in her armoury.

'Have you...?' Her voice broke but she forced herself to go on. 'Have you stopped to ask yourself whether a puppy will compensate me for not being able to bear your children, Grant? Will you give me one every two years, say?'

A sudden white shade appeared around his mouth and she tensed because for the first time ever she was afraid of him, but what he said took her by surprise...

He said in a hard, steely voice, 'Do you know what Lisa's children mean to her, Briony? Not nearly as much as her career; in fact they meant hardly anything at all as babies—they might just as well have *been* puppies. Now, though, that they're graduating from little savages, as she puts it, she doesn't mind showing them off——'

'Stop,' she whispered. 'I'm not Lisa.'

'Then you'd better find a man to give you children, Briony. Perhaps when you've got that out of your system we could—do a deal.'

I don't believe this... The thought ran through her mind. I knew he was hard but not this hard —— Oh, God, what to do?

It was the image of her mother appearing suddenly in her mind that gave her the strength to do what she did. She thought of Serena battling over the years to raise two children, and refusing several offers of marriage which would have made life easier for her in a lot of ways, although perhaps not for her daughters in any but a material sense. And for some reason that image made it very clear to her that if she couldn't feel comfortable with herself, couldn't square things with herself, it was better to opt out before she tore herself apart...

'All right,' she said quietly. 'Not that I'll be doing just that but...' She shrugged and tried to veil the tears.

'Briony —— '

'Grant,' she whispered, 'if you have any feeling for me at all...just let me go. It couldn't work; I couldn't make it work the way you want it.'

'Well, what did you have in mind?' he said curtly. 'Working *for* me still?'

She bit her lip.

'Purely as boss and employee?' he said with soft but unmistakable satire. 'That might be harder than you think, Briony.' He moved his hands on her but there was a glitter in his eyes that was hard and raking. 'For instance, will you be able to forget how very much you enjoy it when I——' he slipped her zip down again '——undress you quite slowly like this?' He brought his hands up to her shoulders and eased the dress down. 'Forget how you move when you're lying under me?' he said barely audibly. 'Believe me, Briony, *working* under me won't be nearly as pleasurable.' His gaze lingered on the curves of her breasts beneath her bra where the dress had slipped down, then he looked into her eyes and the expression in his was devastatingly insolent and mocking.

She paled but the colour of her eyes deepened to a brilliant angry blue. 'You think I couldn't do it?' she asked huskily. 'Just watch me, Grant Goodman.' And she wrenched herself free.

He let her go but raised an eyebrow as she all but tore her dress off then sat on the bed and removed her tights, and this time his gaze lingered on her long legs but there was a glint of amusement in them. And he drawled, 'I'm watching, Briony. Are you planning to strip before my eyes? One wonders what's going through your mind if so, but I'm in no way averse to it, of course,' he assured her lazily.

She gritted her teeth and got up to march over to her bag where she pulled out a tracksuit she hadn't unpacked and a pair of thick socks. 'It's probably just as well you don't know what's going through my mind, Grant.' She got into the tracksuit as quickly as she could then stood on one leg to pull a sock on. 'Because you might not like it at all.' She pulled the other sock on then strode over to where her clothes were hanging and in one sweep pulled them all out and carted them back to the bag, where she threw them in.

'Briony, you're being ridiculous,' he said drily.

'No, I'm not,' she countered as her cosmetics and toiletries met the same fate as her clothes. She looked around, collected her shoes and slung them in, except for one pair, which she slipped on, then reached for her handbag and her bomber jacket. She stopped at last and faced him defiantly. 'I may be some of the things you believe I am, Grant, and you may have reasons for being the way you are—I'm sure we all do—but it's not *ridiculous* to walk away from a man like you, it's only common sense. Moreover I shall have no trouble working *for* you now I've come to my senses, but just don't so much as lay a finger on me ever again!'

He contemplated her thoughtfully; in fact, she thought, and it made her even angrier, he looked entirely at ease. He'd made no effort to button up his shirt, his hair was still awry, but as he stood there looking at her with his hands shoved casually into his pockets it was not hard to see why this man had achieved what he had out of one disaster-prone cattle station. There was the authority of a powerful will stamped all over him, as well as the authority of a man who would always have women eating out of his hand... But not *this* one, she thought, and said grimly, 'So goodbye for the time being, Grant; I'm sure——'

'One moment, Briony,' he broke in coolly. 'I know you delight in giving free rein to your temper but this *is* ridiculous. It will prove nothing to storm out of here like this and drive yourself back to Heath House in a rage. It's also raining, in case you hadn't noticed—you could drive yourself over a cliff.'

'Your concern is touching,' she said scornfully, 'but nevertheless that's what I'm about to do —— '

'Drive yourself over a cliff? My dear Briony, one of the things I'm not worthy of is that.'

'*No*!' She glared at him infuriatedly. 'You know very well what I mean—oh!' She ground her teeth. 'I'm just... going.'

'You're also crying,' he commented.

'I never cry for long, Grant.' She tilted her chin at him and disregarded the tears streaming down her cheeks. 'I don't think you're worthy of that, either. Have fun!' And she swept up her bags and swept out.

Mercifully there was no one about when she arrived back at Heath House so she was able to slip into her suite unnoticed or, if not that, without having to talk to anyone. She locked herself in, leant back against the door and to her horror discovered she was still crying silent tears, and it took a brandy to stem them. But even when she was calm at last and staring into the fire there was the realisation to cope with that she'd flung down an impossible gauntlet. How could she go on working for him?

'I must have been mad,' she murmured to herself. 'I *am* mad. One moment I believe I love him as I could never love another man and then I hate him—I've got to be wrong somewhere down the line. I just hope and pray it's the hate, not the love that's the right instinct. But in the meantime what am I going to do?'

The decision was taken out of her hands to an extent the following morning when she discovered that Linda had succumbed to bronchitis, that one of the housemaids had sprained her ankle and one of the waitresses had conceived a sudden and violent dislike of her job and her surroundings and had taken herself 'back to civilisation', as she'd put it. So it was an anxious, harried and sickly staff she'd found, who'd breathed a collective sigh of relief at her return and had too much on their minds to wonder why she should be back a day early. Oliver had greeted her ecstatically and it had dismayed her that the sudden tendency to tears she'd acquired had come back to plague her at the sight of his joy. Fortunately Linda had been feeling too sick to notice.

So it was an exhausting day as she re-grouped her staff as best she could and coped with an eighty-per-cent occupancy. And she fell into bed that night too tired to think much and grateful for it. One thought she couldn't help, though, was when Grant would come...

He came the next day during lunchtime and found her alone in the office, manning Reception. She looked up not because she'd heard anything but because some sixth sense caused her neck to prickle, and it came to her that he might have been there for a couple of minutes. He was leaning casually against the door-frame, watching her steadily. Nor did that steady hazel gaze flicker as she first of all gasped with surprise then felt herself blushing, and finally the colour drained away, leaving her slightly pale. To make matters worse, she tried to say something but no words would come, although he waited politely.

Then he straightened and said, 'Well, Briony, what's it to be today? More of the same or has a period of sober reflection changed your mind at all?' He closed the door but didn't sit down.

She closed her eyes briefly. 'No, I haven't changed my mind,' she said barely audibly, and swallowed as she watched him run his hand idly over the surface of Linda's desk and recalled exactly how it felt to have him run his hands over her body. 'Nor —— ' she had to clear her throat and clench her hands in her lap as she tried to banish all those treacherous kind of thoughts '—have I had much time for any kind of reflection,' she added with an effort. 'We're short-staffed by three at the moment, although I do have two replacements arriving tomorrow, hopefully.' And she told him about it, although not in any detail apart from mentioning Linda.

He said merely, 'I see,' and sat down in Linda's chair. She waited stiffly as he moved one or two things on the desk then sat back comfortably. 'So,' he murmured, and their gazes clashed, 'if you've had no time to think things through, is there the hope that once this set of crises is past you might see things my way? Is that what you're telling me?'

'Not at all,' she said huskily, clenching her fists again but this time from a desire to restrain herself from throwing things. 'I don't need time to think about that——'

'About us in the personal sense, the very personal, intimate sense, and what it will be like allowing some other man to make love to you?'

'Stop it, Grant,' she said unevenly, her breathing becoming ragged and patches of colour reappearing on her cheeks and throat. 'Only a bastard would do this to me...'

He smiled dispassionately. 'Are you expecting me to be gentlemanly about it all, Briony? Don't you think that when a man and woman have done the kind of things we've done together the need for anything but bare honesty is a little superfluous?'

'No, I don't think that,' she said very quietly. 'In fact I think your bare honesty is something else altogether—perhaps hurt pride? But whatever,' she continued resolutely, 'what I have had time to have some reservations about is continuing to work for you —— '

'You were the one who thought it would be no problem,' he reminded her.

She bit her lip. 'I was angry,' she confessed.

He looked at her wryly. 'You could become a lot angrier,' he murmured. 'Don't forget you have a tendency to go about punching washing machines when you're—frustrated in that particular way,' he said with the kind of gentleness that was a total insult.

Briony stood up. 'And that does it,' she replied crisply. 'I'll continue, Mr Goodman, and you may do your damnedest. Would you be so kind as to let me know how long you plan to stay, and would you then let me get on with my work?'

He lay back lazily and let his gaze drift over her thoughtfully. She was wearing her grey skirt and white jacket. 'Two nights, Briony,' he said idly. 'But I bumped into some friends in Strahan this morning and I invited them to dinner tonight—they're staying at Cradle Mountain Lodge but I thought, if you wouldn't mind, we'd use the private dining-room. There'll be six of us. By the way, that's the only outfit I've seen you wear that doesn't

altogether become you, although of course,'
he shrugged, 'I'm speaking from a preference
for seeing you wear nothing at all.' And he
stood up and strolled out.

'Briony, I'm short-staffed, as you very well
know. Now a party in the private dining-room
needs a waitress on its own!' Peter Marsden
removed his chef's hat and crunched it deliberately between his big hands.

'You tell that to Mr Goodman, Peter,'
Briony said tartly.

'Why don't *you*?' Chef Marsden stopped
and looked at her piercingly.

Briony felt the colour rising beneath her
skin but she took a deep breath and said
evenly, 'Look, here's what we'll do. We'll put
Marcia on to serve them and I'll take her place
in the main dining-room. But I'll set the
private room up. What's on the menu
tonight?'

He told her.

'Sounds fine. I'll get to work.'

An hour later she stood back to admire her
handiwork in the private dining-room and
couldn't fault it. The glasses and silver
gleamed, the pink damask cloth and napkins

were perfectly starched and smooth and the flowers on the table and sideboard looked lovely. And she was confident that Marcia was their most accomplished waitress, as well as being an attractive woman in her thirties. Then she glanced at her watch and found she had a bare twenty minutes to shower and change before the dinner gong sounded.

She was back in Reception in fifteen minutes, wearing a blue gathered skirt and a matching jumper with a white satin, laced-trimmed collar—there was no point in her wearing the pretty uniform the waitresses wore; most people knew who she was anyway. Fortunately, Grant strolled into the area just as his friends arrived, two middle-aged couples and a vibrant, dark-haired girl of about twenty who was a daughter of one of the couples, she guessed, and who was obviously delighted to be in his company. But he did introduce them to her briefly before taking them into the lounge for an aperitif. She couldn't help wondering how different it might have been if she'd agreed to be his mistress—would he have included her in the party, and how would he have introduced her then, for example?

Minutes later, as the hungry horde descended on the dining-room, she had no more time to think those kind of thoughts. Indeed it was ten o'clock, after she'd supervised the feeding of the possums et cetera, which Grant had brought his guests to watch and stood back watching her enigmatically, before she'd been able to relax at all.

She'd tidied up the reception desk, looked around, then retreated to the office where a supper tray and coffee waited for her.

She was halfway through her meal, the first she'd had since a very light lunch on the run, when he came in and closed the door behind him.

Briony raised her napkin to her lips and pushed her plate away. 'Mr Goodman,' she said formally. 'I hope your dinner was up to expectations.'

'It was excellent, thank you,' he said quietly. 'But you should have told me your troubles with staff affected the dining-room.'

She shrugged. 'We managed well enough.'

'Only with you working a sixteen-hour day.'

'That's what the job is all about sometimes.' She smiled mechanically. 'Anyway, I'm as strong as a horse and by tomorrow we should be back to normal. Linda is feeling a lot better.'

He said nothing for a moment, then, 'You don't look as strong as a horse at the moment.'

Briony grimaced and poured herself a cup of coffee. 'Would you like to see the forward bookings? They're pretty good considering it's getting towards winter now.'

'I'll take your word for it, thank you.' He stood up. 'Why don't you go to bed?'

'I will, when I've taken Oliver for a run.'

He looked for a moment as if he was going to take issue with this but as she summoned a last weary yet defiant glance at him his mouth hardened and he turned on his heel and walked out.

'Oh, Ollie,' she whispered later as they walked back through the cold dark night, 'what am I going to do?'

Predictably the little dog didn't answer but he licked her hand lovingly.

Linda was back on deck the next morning and obviously burning with curiosity now she felt better, but after several unsuccessful attempts to steer the conversation Grant Goodman's way she gave up. What gossip was flying about the place Briony didn't even bother to wonder about, but she couldn't help knowing she was both at her best—and her worst. Crisp, businesslike, supremely efficient but entirely unapproachable. That it should all boil over into a row with Lucien was perhaps entirely predictable. It was supremely unfortunate that Grant happened to be unseen but in earshot...

'Lucien,' Briony said, coming across him outside the kitchen, 'I'd like to speak to you, please. There's been a complaint. Would you come to my suite now?'

But Lucien put his hands on his hips and regarded her in a superior fashion. 'Complaint? About me? Who dares to do this? I am the best!'

'You may be the best guide but there are other things involved.'

'So tell me here and now, Briony,' he said, and added scornfully, 'I am no schoolboy to be called to the office, and by a woman!'

Briony breathed deeply and said coldly, 'Very well. If you would like any of the staff who happen to be about to hear, so be it. In one of the guest questionnaires I was going through this morning the comment was made by a gentleman who left two days ago that the only thing that had spoilt his stay at Heath House was *your* overly familiar treatment of his wife.'

Lucien snorted. 'If I, Lucien du Plessis, was familiar, Briony, she was undoubtedly asking for it and this man should ask himself not who is this but *why* is this? Because if he cannot keep her happy in his bed her eyes will always roam. I know about these women!'

'I'm sure you do, Lucien,' Briony retorted, 'but, be that as it may, while you're working *here* you will keep your eyes and your hands off all wives or girlfriends despite any provocation, should that be the case or—should it not. Do you understand me, Lucien?'

'You are threatening me, Briony?' he responded with dangerous ingenuousness.

'Yes, I'm threatening you, Lucien,' she said through her teeth. 'One more complaint and you're out!'

He smiled at her insolently. 'Don't think I don't know why *this* is, Briony. You are suffering from problems of the same nature yourself, is that not so? Monsieur Goodman has withdrawn the privilege of sharing his bed with you, has he not? I, on the other hand——'

He got no further as Briony slapped his good-looking face a resounding blow and would have done so again, as Lucien growled and brought his hands up to retaliate, had not Grant Goodman said from behind them, 'Lucien, *mon ami*, I wouldn't if I were you. In fact *I* will see you in the office in half an hour. Briony, come with me.'

'Are you going to tell me I shouldn't have done it?'

She swung on her heel to confront Grant Goodman as he closed the door of her suite, her eyes still glittering with rage.

He said drily with his hand still on the doorknob, 'There are slightly more diplomatic ways of going about these things——'

'There are *not*! And shall I tell you why? Because you're all the same. Men,' she said disgustedly and sat down suddenly.

'And you are dangerously overwrought and probably overtired,' he replied evenly.

'I wonder whose fault that is?' She laughed coldly. 'No, don't answer. It's *never* been of any concern to you that you've put me in an impossible position.'

'Briony,' he said patiently, 'we can discuss this from a business point of view or a private one. You choose.'

'And if that isn't a cop-out I've never heard one,' she said agitatedly, then took several deep breaths as his expression hardened. 'All right, let's discuss it from a business angle,' she said with an effort. 'Lucien is a very good guide. From the point of view that he takes good care of everyone, takes no risks, is a bit of a weather prophet in his own right, is the kind of character people love and re-member—and can charm the pants off everyone,' she said bleakly, 'you can only call him a success. But when husbands start com-plaining about him—and, to be honest, he's broken not a few hearts among the staff, too—you have to weigh it all up and, to my mind, he's becoming a liability.'

'Then you don't believe he's merely the re-cipient of the kind of admiration some bored wives would bestow on him in the natural course of events? You can't blame the bloke for that.'

'Far be it from me to do that!' she said with patent scorn.

'Briony ——'

'No, Grant, it's more than that. He said *himself* if he was familiar with this woman it was only because he was being encouraged. If he can't withstand encouragement from married women guests, heaven alone knows what havoc he could create one day.'

'You're right,' Grant said thoughtfully.

Briony shrugged, then her shoulders sagged. 'On the other hand, it could take a little while to replace him.'

'How do you think you would cope with him after this?'

'I should have thought he made that very obvious just now,' she said with irony.

'Ah,' Grant murmured, 'but I hadn't made my position quite clear on the subject—just now.'

Briony stared at him. 'What difference will that make?'

'Once he understands from me that his job is on the line, he might see the light.'

Briony opened her mouth, closed it, then said wearily, 'Much as I'd love to, I don't doubt it. All the same he will never have much respect for *me* again.'

'Do you think he's entitled to respect you less?'

'I don't really give a damn about his opinions or —— ' She broke off and bit her lip then coloured as he looked at her quizzically. 'So long as he keeps them to himself,' she added, and stood up abruptly. 'All right! I shouldn't have slapped his face, and perhaps I hadn't until now made it perfectly clear to him that he was not to encourage guests. So if you'd like to give him another chance, go ahead. You own the place after all. I'd just love to be a fly on the wall when you discuss it with him—how will you handle the subject of my behaving the way I am because of *you* withdrawing the privilege of sharing your bed?'

'You needn't be a fly on the wall.' He opened the door and stared at her penetratingly. 'Be my guest.'

'Lucien, we have a problem,' Grant Goodman said coolly. 'In fact we have two. And I've asked Briony to sit in on this discussion because she had the feeling we might indulge in one of those men-to-men kind of chats where women are rather degraded.'

Lucien, who was sitting at Linda's desk while Briony sat at her own and Grant leaned idly against the wall, started to look amused, met a cold hazel gaze and changed his mind.

'So let me make it perfectly plain in the first place that Briony is in charge here and that I respect her judgement completely in these matters.' He paused and subjected Lucien to a laser-like glance that could have passed through a brick wall. And for the first time ever Briony saw Lucien look a little discomfited.

'Which brings me to my second point,' Grant went on. 'When Briony tells me that you're becoming a liability despite the fact that you're an excellent guide I believe her. So, again, let me set out the situation. There is perhaps a time-honoured perception that some positions in hotels and resorts et cetera, are somewhat ambiguous; that the tennis coach or the ski instructor for example can also be a gigolo in disguise. That is *not* the case here——'

Lucien made a protesting sound but Grant held up his hand. 'On the other hand, there are people who simply aren't suited to this kind of job by virtue of its isolation and, while that in itself is no crime, it would be foolish for anyone to continue here if it was a problem for them.'

Lucien opened his mouth then dropped his gaze and apparently decided to hold his peace.

'To sum up, then,' Grant said after a moment, 'Briony has the ultimate authority here, Lucien, so if you resent that in any way you should consider your position very carefully, and attached female guests are off-limits.'

What Lucien then did took Briony completely by surprise. He rose up from his chair with dignity, looked first at her, then at Grant and said, '*Mon ami*, to admire women is of the second nature to me—to lose this job, no, that is not what I wish. *Furthermore ——* ' but his glance was still dignified as he looked at Grant '——I, Lucien du Plessis, have never accepted any payment for bringing joy to a lady; their pleasure alone is reward enough for me, but if some are off-limits,' he shrugged, '*c'est la vie*! And —— ' he turned to Briony '——there are many things I admire about you, *mademoiselle*. Many things. Perhaps it would be the good thing if we try to understand each other better from now on, *n'est-ce pas*?'

Briony actually surprised herself. She stood up and held out her hand to him. 'I would like to try, Lucien.'

'You're amused?' Grant queried idly, a few moments after the door had closed behind Lucien, and Briony was still smiling.

'I can't help it.' She strove for composure. 'Can't you see the funny side of it? I mean— I actually thought it was a very gallant gesture and Lucien surprised me, but it did have its funny side. Didn't it?'

He grimaced. 'I may not be in a laughing mood. Or perhaps I'm just on the same side of the fence as Lucien.' He shrugged.

Briony sobered completely and found she felt a little light-headed, which might have accounted for her mirth, or might not have. In point of fact, she thought, I don't know what to think or say or do any more... She closed her eyes and rubbed her brow. 'Well, I have to thank you,' she said uncertainly, 'for solving that the way you did. Of course, only time will tell how it succeeds but...' She gestured and added laconically, 'Thanks, anyway.'

He gazed at her steadily for a long moment. 'I'm glad you appreciate it,' he said finally and, for some reason not apparent to her, his eyes were curiously mocking. 'But I must tell you my first instinct was to solve it quite differently.'

She looked at him blankly.

'Mmm...' he said thoughtfully. 'My first instinct was to knock Lucien out cold when he referred to our sharing beds in the way he did, and to forcibly remove you *back* to my bed there and then, thereby putting an end to this—nonsense.' His gaze raked her from head to toe for a brief instant then returned to thoughtfulness.

Briony gasped and felt herself go hot and cold.

'My second instinct, however,' he went on imperturbably, 'was that things might have degenerated into an all-out brawl—in other words that you might not have appreciated that, Briony, and it seems I was right,' he concluded gently.

'Might—certainly not the second bit,' she said disjointedly. 'That's —— ' She stopped.

'Blackmail? Bribery? No, hackneyed, of course!' he marvelled. 'How dense of me.'

Briony stilled and stared at him, unable to gauge his mood, hoping against hope for a brief, mad moment that he was teasing her, then knowing with a chill feeling around her heart that he wasn't. 'What I don't understand is what this has to do with . . . to do with my refusing to be your mistress,' she said huskily, at last. 'You've lost me somewhere along the line, Grant, I have to confess.'

'It's quite simple,' he drawled. 'It really has to do with the fact that we are helping no one with this state of affairs, Briony. Least of all ourselves.'

She took a breath then said carefully, 'Time may help to heal all that.'

'Do you really believe it?' He strolled over to her. 'I wonder. If on the other hand you think that time will wring a wedding-ring out of me, don't be disappointed if it doesn't.' And he touched one finger carelessly to the point of her chin. 'By the way, I'm leaving this afternoon.'

'Are you?' she said through stiff lips. 'Goodbye, then, Grant.'

He smiled but not with his eyes. 'Goodbye, Briony, but since we've discussed time once or twice lately let's not leave out that wonderful, hackneyed old saying about the things we might do *for old times' sake.*' And he took her into his arms, kissed her deliberately and lingeringly, then added as her eyes glittered with a mixture of tears and anger, 'Goodbye, Briony. May this have all blown over by the next time we meet.'

CHAPTER TEN

'BRIONY—what are you doing?'

Briony raised her head from her desk where she was surrounded by a sea of paperwork and stared steadily at Linda. 'I think you must know, Linda,' she said quietly after a moment.

'But... are you just going to walk out?'

'Not entirely. I'm getting everything as up to date as I can for you. But I plan to leave tomorrow... If there's one thing you could do for me, it would be not to alert anyone until after I've gone—I know that will involve some lies for you but ——'

Linda gestured impatiently. 'As if I wouldn't tell a few lies for a friend! But don't do this, Briony, I beg of you. There must be some other way to sort things out!'

'There's not,' Briony said steadily.

'There has to be. You *love* him, don't you?'

Briony sat back with a grimace. 'What makes you so sure of that?'

'I saw you,' Linda said sadly and shook her head. 'I mean, it was obvious from the moment you two laid eyes on each other that there was an electric charge between you. Then there was how you were when you —— ' she gestured delicately '——and how you are now.'

'Yes, well, unfortunately it's not at all clear to me whether I love him or hate him, but one thing is clear—he suspected my motives right from the beginning and nothing I've done since has made him change his mind. In other words, he'd be quite happy to sleep with me but that's about all. Oh, well, to be a business partner too —— '

'That may have to do with his first marriage, Briony,' Linda said reproachfully.

'It may indeed and it may all have been a storm in a teacup,' Briony said briskly. 'We didn't actually get the chance to know each other very well, so —— '

'Then why don't you stay and at least give him a chance to know you better?'

Briony stared across the office at nothing in particular. 'Because I do believe he won't change,' she said very quietly. 'Linda —— ' she refocused on the other girl and her gaze softened. '——I'm going; I have to. I haven't felt right with myself over this and, whatever his problems are, if he can't at least understand that—well, it's never going to be any good.'

Linda stared at her then she said quietly, 'And does he know the truth about why you left Sydney, Briony?'

'No.' She frowned. 'Do you?'

Linda hesitated. 'I told you about my source in Sydney, didn't I?'

Briony smiled faintly. 'You certainly did.'

'Well, it's her contention that Nick Semple is a real bastard, that he cheats on his wife and it was *much* more likely that he was the one who chased you. She just can't understand why you accepted all the blame.'

Briony blinked then shrugged. 'It doesn't matter, Linda.'

'It *does*. You said Mr Goodman suspected your motives! If you don't *tell* him ——'

Briony stood up. 'I doubt if it would make one bit of difference, other than harming someone totally innocent, but as a matter of fact I did try to a couple of times. He—didn't really want to know. Which used to puzzle me,' she said more to herself, 'but doesn't really now. No, Linda —— '

'Well, where are you going?' Linda said with a shade of desperation.

Briony smiled at her affectionately then crossed to her desk to give her a quick hug. 'I'll let you know,' she said, and her voice clogged up with sudden emotion. 'And thank you for being such a friend.'

Six months later, Briony sat down in a shady corner of the garden and was for some reason reminded of Linda; she found herself wondering how she was. Because she never had got in touch, although she often hoped devoutly that Linda would understand why. But then again, why? she asked herself. Did I imagine Grant would find out where I was from her and rush here to—whatever? Well, she answered herself, perhaps you did, which was why you sometimes had to forcibly restrain yourself from picking up the phone. And that brings us to another question, Briony. When are you going to forget Grant Goodman?

She laid her head back and closed her eyes against the shade-dappled sunlight. And trembled because sometimes it was still as if he were right there with her. She could see in her mind's eye the way his hair fell, his hands, she could picture him climbing Cradle Mountain and feel him handling her body... She always tried to tell herself to remember the worst things about him, such as his last taunt about wringing a wedding-ring from him, but as the months had progressed she'd begun to miss him almost intolerably at times. It was as if her anger had been unsustainable faced with life without him.

Which, she sometimes thought bitterly, was a cruel thing to have happen to her when she knew she'd done the right thing. But, love him or hate him, she now knew that without him she was a different person. She was lonely, she was often lack-lustre and she felt as if she'd lost half of herself. She didn't even have the ambition to find herself a more challenging job than the one she had, which she'd accepted on the spur of the moment as a stop-gap and which was in an out-of-the-way place to make it difficult to find her.

She smiled sadly as she wondered what Grant would think of her, buried in a very small but historic midland Tassie town, running a four-room although also historic guest house where she did everything apart from having a weekly cleaner. She made the beds, she provided breakfast, she ran the gift shop attached to it and she tended the garden.

She opened her eyes with a grimace and looked around at said garden, which was certainly beautiful with a lovely green lawn and all sorts of spring flowers starting to bloom. In fact the whole place was rather lovely, and the town, albeit so small, was the centre of one of the finest wool-producing areas of Australia and was graced by some lovely old buildings and churches. It had seemed to her to be a good place to lick her wounds and try to gather some serenity from its peaceful, unhurried graciousness. Now it seemed, though, that she lacked the will even to move on and that her wounds might never heal...

'No!' She sat up abruptly, and Oliver, who was lying beside her, sprang up and put a questioning paw on her lap. She smoothed his head ruefully. 'It's all right, old son. I was just feeling a bit maudlin—what say we go for a really long walk?'

The next morning she decided to make some scones. She had two elderly ladies staying who made an annual pilgrimage to the area where they'd grown up and she thought she'd give them a bang-up morning tea. And it was with floury hands and a streak of flour across her forehead that she heard Oliver barking in the back garden. Then he stopped and it crossed her mind that the front doorbell must be playing up again so whoever it was had come round the back. But she froze as she heard a man's voice and heard him say to the dog, 'You may not know this, mate, but I was the bloke who rescued you from a pet shop. How's your mistress?'

And that was how Grant Goodman found her as he knocked briefly on the open back door then stepped over the threshold into the sun-warmed, old-fashioned kitchen. Found her with a tea-towel tied around her middle and wearing old tracksuit trousers, old sand-shoes and a faded yellow blouse... And her mouth fell open, her eyes widened and she clutched the table suddenly as the kitchen whirled briefly around her then steadied.

'Briony,' he said quietly, his hazel gaze taking in the way her colour receded then returned a bit, 'I didn't mean to surprise you quite as much—are you all right?'

'No...yes! I'm fine,' she said weakly, and rubbed the back of her wrist on her cheek, leaving more flour on her face. 'What...what are *you* doing here?' she added foolishly, then swallowed convulsively. 'I mean...' But she couldn't go on.

'I'm here to see you,' he said in the same quiet voice. 'I've been searching for you for months.'

'*Why*?'

He smiled, but not as if he was amused. 'Why do you think?'

Briony stared at him. He was formally dressed in a suit and tie but apart from some faint new lines around his mouth which she didn't remember he looked exactly the same— tall, strong and impressive.

She switched her gaze away and groped for a chair. 'I don't know what to think,' she said hollowly, and put her hands to her face. Then she looked at them frustratedly, jumped up and began to stride across to the sink.

He put out a hand and caught her wrist as she went past.

'Grant ——— '

'Look,' he said gently, 'why don't you finish what you're doing and why don't you let me make us a cup of tea in the meantime?'

She trembled because he was close enough for her to see the flecks of green in his hazel eyes, to breathe in the essence of him. She closed her eyes. Then she said abruptly, 'OK. Kettle's over there and everything for tea is on the dresser. But I must warn you, I'm not ——— '

'Going to be a pushover?' he suggested evenly.

Briony pulled her wrist free and returned to her scone mixture with her mouth set mutinously, but also incipient tears threatening. Grant studied her bent head and kneading hands for a long moment then he pulled his jacket off and went over to the kettle.

And they said nothing until the scones were in the oven, she'd piled her equipment into the sink and rinsed her hands, and tea was made.

'Here.' He pulled out a chair for her and sat down himself. 'I hope you like it strong.'

'I do. Thanks.' She stared down at her cup then lifted her frowning gaze to his. 'How did you find me?'

'Your mother.'

Briony's eyebrows flew up. 'I don't believe it,' she whispered. 'She would have let me know!'

'I asked her not to. I explained the whole situation to her, and she agreed. In fact, if she hadn't remarried and changed her name I would have found you a lot sooner.'

'Do you mean to say you've *browbeaten* my own mother into —— ?'

'There was no browbeating involved at all. I simply went to see her and placed all the facts before her. *She* made the decision to tell me——'

'I can imagine!'

'I don't think you can and before you work yourself up any further, Briony,' he said with a pointed little look, 'let's get one thing out of the way for once and for all—Nick Semple.

Now I know there were times when I didn't make it easy for you and times when I didn't want to know, and I'll tell you why —— '

'I know why,' she said huskily, and sipped some too hot tea.

He shrugged. 'All right, you tell me.'

Their gazes locked. Briony took a breath and said, 'So that you could always hold me at arm's length because you had that doubt about me.'

He grimaced. 'You're right.'

Her lips parted.

'Which we'll go into in a moment,' he went on. 'What I don't understand is why you felt any guilt, why you took the fall for it and why you let me go on thinking—or doubting,' he said with a sort of grim mockery that amazed her because it was obviously self-directed.

She blinked. 'So you don't believe any more that I —— ?'

'No, I don't. Once I—came back to some sanity, I just couldn't believe it of you. So why, Briony? Was it your way of trying to hold *me* at arm's length?'

She sighed and stood up and took her cup over to the window. 'Grant,' she said at last,

'I will always feel some guilt but, for what it's worth, this is how it happened. Only, before I tell you, I have to have your promise you won't—do anything about it.'

His eyes narrowed as if he was contemplating a mystery that was unfolding. Then he focused on her. 'I promise.'

'When I first met Nick, I'd just been promoted. It was a big job and quite a step up the ladder. He was my immediate superior as well as a member of the Semple family——' she turned to him and grimaced '—and we worked together a lot. And when he put out the customary feelers so many men do I made it very plain to him I wasn't interested for at least two very good reasons: he was married and he was my boss. He took it with surprisingly good grace, or so I thought. But in fact I was later to realise that he only became much more subtle.'

'Go on.'

'And so one day,' she said bleakly, 'I found myself having lunch with him in the hotel restaurant—I mean, it was perfectly innocent; we'd both been working flat out all morning but because he can be amusing, because he can be likeable, because I'd got to know him fairly well and —— ' she gestured a little helplessly '—and dealt with him nearly every day of my life, it slipped into being a social thing, instead of business, boss and employee et cetera. And anyone looking on would have assumed it was a—social lunch.

'In fact that's what alerted me. When he got up to go I realised some of the staff were looking at us strangely, and it dawned on me that the odd coffee in the coffee shop, lunch and so on had started to mount up. So, a little red light flashed in my brain and I began to wonder if it was all quite harmless, the way he'd sort of gone out of his way to lull me into a false sense of security but at the same time made very sure we were seen together a lot and—had got to know each other rather well, for want of a better way to put it,' she said drily.

'Which, of course, is exactly what he'd done?'

'As events later proved, yes, Grant,' she said tonelessly. 'Because when I then...tried to disengage and keep things on a strictly business footing he—first of all he told me about all his problems with Angelique and he told me that their marriage was little more than in name only, that their disenchantment was mutual and so on. When I indicated that I wasn't interested anyway, he turned somewhat nasty. He threatened me with dismissal, and he pointed out all the lonely hours we'd spent working together and how we could have been doing *anything* . . . and I suddenly began to see how, with little effort, a malicious man could make that look . . . very suspect. In fact I began to see more; I began to see that the other Semples, his mother and his uncle particularly, were starting to treat me very coolly.'

'What did you do?'

Briony put her empty teacup down on the table. 'I didn't know what to do at first. I couldn't believe I'd been fool enough to let it happen but —— ' She stopped and sighed. 'I was so wrapped up in the job, so determined to keep going up the ladder,' she said bitterly, 'I honestly didn't wake up until it was too late. When I did, I decided there was only one thing to do, and that was confront him and tell him he was employing a form of sexual harassment, that he was virtually blackmailing me to sleep with him to keep my job—and I would expose him for it unless it all ceased immediately. That was the day,' she said with an effort, 'Angelique walked in on us.'

'He'd never touched you before?'

'No. But when I started my spiel he grabbed me, pinned me to the wall and started to kiss me. And although I fought like a maniac he was too strong for me, and when Angelique opened the door I was out of breath and exhausted, but it obviously looked as if it was because I—was a willing party.'

'My dear,' Grant said with compassion, 'why on earth didn't you ——?'

'Expose him to his own wife?'

'Well, to *someone*.'

'I'll never forget her face,' Briony said slowly. 'I'd never actually met her before although I'd seen her and—of course I don't have to explain Angelique to you, do I? But just to see her and the way she dressed was to know that she was young and probably quite naïve but, that aside, what I saw in her eyes— the disbelief, the stunned horror, the de- spair ——' she swallowed '—told me that he'd *lied* about her. She wasn't disenchanted with him at all, she adored him if anything, and it was as if her whole world was tumbling about her in ruins. To this day, and perhaps always, I will feel guilty, Grant, for, however unwittingly—and it *was*, but all the same—causing that. For being so wrapped in my ambitions and my career that I didn't see what was happening.'

'So you gave in without a fight?'

She grimaced. 'I still might not have because I still didn't, at that point, really understand how the decks were stacked against me. But Angelique fled in tears, Nick chased after her and half an hour later I was summoned to appear before his mother and uncle. They put it to me that I had trapped Nick, I had used all sorts of feminine wiles to attract him against his better judgement, I'd blackmailed him with exposure and it had been my ultimate intention to break up his marriage when I'd got him so besotted he wouldn't be able to resist me.

'Do you know, for a moment I was tempted to wonder if I'd wandered into a madhouse? And nothing I said made the slightest impression.' She shook her head. 'Of course at the time I didn't know what part you, through Angelique, played in it all. What did dawn on me, though, was that I was hitting my head against a brick wall, that that was exactly what Nick would be telling Angelique—that I'd trapped him et cetera, and finally I told them to believe what they liked, I was quitting anyway, and I stormed out.

'But after a period of sober reflection it also dawned on me that there wasn't a great deal I could do, other than try to take him to court for sexual harassment. And, do you know, there were two people I just couldn't bring myself to put through that? Myself and Angelique.'

'Briony——'

'Do you believe me, Grant?'

'Yes, it *had* to be something like that; I was just too—deliberately blind, perhaps, to acknowledge it. So all the time you were protecting Angelique, in fact?'

'In a sense, yes,' she said sombrely.

'You didn't think that never to know how guilty Nick was could in fact harm her more than help her?'

Briony sighed and sat down again. 'It's all very well to think those things, but to actually bring yourself to go to a woman who believed the sun shone out of her husband and tell her what a bastard he is, is a different matter. And there was the possibility that he might have got enough of a fright to reform—who knows? That's what I hoped might have happened.'

'And that's why you were afraid I might stick my oar in once I knew the truth?'

'Yes... But don't imagine it was all as noble and self-sacrificing as it sounds. For weeks after I walked out I combed every avenue I could think of to clear my name. I went to see a solicitor, I spoke to friends and colleagues—but I finally came to the conclusion that it could cost me an awful lot of money to take the matter to court and there was no way I could guarantee the outcome. So, in the end, but with a lot of bitterness, believe me, I decided to cut my losses and—start again. But once I did that I...I suppose,' she said slowly, 'and this may sound crazy but I just couldn't forget her face, so I suppose I thought, Well if this helps anyone, perhaps it will help Angelique. I'm not terribly sure how but that's what I've had at the back of my mind ever since. Perhaps it really translates to thinking that if they don't make it, it won't be for lack of trying, although belatedly, on my part...oh!' She jumped up and rescued her scones from the oven. 'Damn.'

'They're still edible,' he said with a crooked grin.

'Only just.' She grimaced.

'Which brings us back to—us,' he said. 'Another cup of tea?'

'Look, I'm due to *serve* tea in about half an hour!' She looked about her, suddenly flustered. 'And I've got a dozen other things to do—would you mind——?' She stopped.

'Would I mind...?'

'Coming back or something,' she said lamely. 'I've nothing on later this afternoon.'

'Why not? I've booked into the pub, as it happens.' He looked at her steadily. 'On the condition that you promise me something— you won't run away again.'

She bit her lip.

'Briony?'

'No, Grant.' Her shoulders sagged. 'But——'

He stood up and reached for his jacket. 'How about four o'clock?'

'That would be—fine.'

He hesitated briefly as their gazes caught and held, then he said simply, 'See you then.'

Briony was incredibly distracted as she served her elderly ladies morning tea and apologised for the darker than usual demeanour of the scones. They assured her later that they'd been delicious but they also asked her a touch anxiously if she was feeling all right.

I must take hold, she told herself as she did her chores, but discovered to her dismay that her hands were shaking. At three o'clock, she took a long shower—there was not the luxury of spas at this establishment—and pondered what to wear. In the end, because the premature spring weather had turned capricious and it was cold and gloomy, she chose a pair of black ski pants and her Fair Isle sweater. But as she did her hair and thought that she looked strained and unvital—even her hair seemed to have lost some of its bounce—her hands started to shake again and she had to sit down.

'Why has he come?' she asked herself aloud for the umpteenth time. 'If it's the same proposition, will I have the strength to say no again? Would he not have just come out and...swept me off my feet otherwise? But he did admit that he'd used his doubts about me and Nick Semple to hold me at arm's length—oh, God, what does that mean?'

Then the doorbell rang and she was amazed to see that it was four o'clock already...

'Come into the guest lounge,' she said brightly when she opened the door. 'My only two guests are out visiting relatives and won't be back until late. Besides, I've lit a fire.'

'Thanks.' He took off his raincoat and revealed a brightly coloured sweater she remembered, and jeans. 'I walked.'

'Well, it's not far. Here we are.'

'Ah.' He walked into the old-fashioned, knick-knack-strewn lounge and immediately seemed to dwarf it; he held his hands out to the fire. 'Tassie weather at its worst,' he said wryly.

'Yes—Grant——' all of a sudden it all boiled up inside her '—tell me why you've come. I...I don't think we need to beat about the bush, do we?'

He straightened and turned to her. 'No. But may I explain some things to *you* first?'

'Well...OK,' she said jerkily. 'Sit down.' And she sat down herself.

He stared into the fire for a moment then lifted his eyes to hers and said, 'You once accused me of making every woman a scapegoat for Lisa's shortcomings, or words to that effect... I think I denied it—I think I actually said I wasn't quite as Freudian as that. I was wrong.'

Her lips parted.

'You see, Lisa used a particular form of blackmail to get her own way. To put it baldly, she used her body; she manipulated my— delight in it and she was quite brazen about it. In other words, she either withheld or bestowed sex on me as a sign of her disapproval or as a reward. But when she was disapproving she did more; she would send out ''come hither'' signals to other men and then watch me to see how it affected me. And gradually she was doing the same to any man who came her way.

'I began to see that that was how she got us all in—directors, co-stars, anything in trousers, and all with that same sultry body language that promised such delight—and I knew it wouldn't be long before she would be unfaithful to me.'

He paused, watched the fire for a moment then lifted his eyes to hers. 'To discover one is in thrall to a woman like that, let alone married to her—well, it can be a particularly unpleasant discovery. To be moved to using brute strength out of sheer frustration and know that she had deliberately driven you to it can provide the makings of a kind of hell... To have your children conceived in a situation like that and then held up to you as a form of ransom can produce wounds that take a long time to heal. So even though I walked away from her in the end, even though I rid myself of... whatever it was that got me in the first place and, much as you tell yourself not all women are like that, well —— ' he gestured '—there's an old saying about women scorned—there should be one about men who've been made a fool of. I think,' he said simply, 'I made a subconscious vow that no woman would ever be able to hold me to ransom in that particular way again.'

'So?' Briony whispered, her eyes huge.

'So ——' he looked away briefly '——when I found myself wanting you the way I did, I immediately tried to rationalise it and I decided that it had to be on my terms or not at all, and my terms were that you should never be allowed to get closer to me than a mistress, and not only that but in a position where I could manipulate *you*. And I told myself this was only good sense—there was, after all, the doubt about you and Nick,' he said drily and looked back into her eyes at last.

A log collapsed in the fireplace in a shower of sparks. Briony licked her lips and wondered if she dared to hope at all. 'Has...has anything changed?' she said, having difficulty making her voice work.

'I regret to say this, but no.' His voice deepened as she tensed visibly. 'I mean, no—don't say anything until I've finished, Briony, because you might not like it much. But nothing changed overnight. In fact I waited for a few months after you left Heath House before I made any attempts to find you. I clung to my theory that you were black-mailing me in your own way and I wondered how long it would be before you drifted back into my life to see how I was coping without you.

'But then things did change. I found that I was missing you unbearably and I began to see that there was not the remotest similarity between the way you'd made love to me and the way Lisa had, and I began to understand that there was no way you could have led Nick on either. And all the time it was beginning to dawn on me that you had *no* intention of coming back. And this is what I really regret to say, Briony, but it was only when I finally acknowledged that that I could draw all those threads together and also acknowledge... how much I *loved* you. And that's when I started to search for you.'

'Why...why —— ' her tongue seemed to trip itself up '—should I mind that?'

'Because if nothing else,' he said sombrely, 'it has to show you what a fool I am, what a proud, arrogant fool.'

'Oh, Grant.' She put her hands to her face to hide her tears.

'But what about you, Briony?' he said gently. 'How do things stand between us for you now? You said to me once that time might...heal things.'

She took her hands away and smiled painfully through her tears. 'Time? Would you really like to know what time has done for me, Grant? I feel like an old woman. I have no zest, no ambition; I couldn't forget you— why do you think I buried myself away here? Why do you think I've been in such a state ever since you knocked at the door? I've been terrified to hope; I —— '

He stood up and pulled her up into his arms. 'I'm so sorry. But I wanted to be able to explain so there could be no misunderstandings ever again. Will you marry me, Briony?'

'Oh, yes...'

'No, don't say it as quickly as that. There are other things you should consider. I'm *still* a workaholic although I've begun to see that work has taken the place of having anyone in my life to love and share things with, but I may never change completely —— '

Briony smiled through her tears. 'As one workaholic to another, I may never either. Had you thought of that? Perhaps the answer is for us to work *together*.'

His lips twisted and he brought his hands up to cup her face. 'That sounds like the perfect solution.' But then he sobered. 'There's also Scott and Hannah. I'm quite sure they've given up any hope of Lisa and me being reconciled but —— ' He paused.

'They tend to regard you as their exclusive property?' She moved her hands on his chest as he nodded rather wryly. 'That's only natural,' she said quietly. 'I will always respect Scott and Hannah and do my best to understand and love them. Will . . . you mind, though, if we have children of our own?'

He lifted a hand and touched her mouth. 'Mind? Put it this way: it wouldn't seem right if we didn't.'

'Do you really mean that, Grant?'

'Of course.' He brushed some fresh tears away with his thumbs. 'That's what loving someone is all about, isn't it?'

Her lips trembled into a smile. 'Then may I say yes now? Because loving you seems to be what I'm all about and——'

'My darling Briony,' he broke in, and held her so close for a moment that she could barely breathe, 'yes, you may.'

The dining-room at Heath House had never looked lovelier, nor, most thought, had the bride. She wore a silvery blue ankle-length dress, her whole family was in attendance, her stepchildren, her mother-in-law and nearly all of her former staff, but three of her staff were looking particularly pleased with themselves—Lucien, Chef Marsden and Linda.

Indeed it was Lucien, dancing with Linda at the reception after the ceremony, who said, 'Is it not great to see Briony looking so happy, *ma chère*?'

Linda sighed luxuriously. 'Wonderful!'

He grinned. 'Still, I feel some sympathy for him. She can be a hard woman to handle!'

Linda stopped dancing and said crossly, 'She certainly had your measure, Lucien du Plessis!' And bit her lip as Briony and Grant danced by.

*　　*　　*

'Do you think I'm a hard woman to handle?'

'Extremely,' Grant murmured, and returned his attention to her body.

Briony smiled. 'I would take issue with that. You seem to be having no trouble handling me at this moment at all.'

'Well, in this respect, you're not actually *that* hard to handle. It's in other respects.'

She ran her fingers through his hair. 'Tell me.'

He sat up, pulled up some pillows and leant back beside her. They were in one of the new chalets; it was dark and wet outside but warm and only firelit within so that leaping shadows played on the wall and turned the colour of her skin where it was bare to the waist to a mixture of gold and rose. 'You're impossible—to live without for one thing.'

She bent her head and kissed his shoulder. 'I have to say the same for you.'

'Happy?'

Briony glanced down at her wedding-ring, which was all she wore other than a sheet, then laid her head back. 'Yes. How about you?'

'More than I thought was possible for a long time. So much more.'

'Oh, Grant.' She trembled and closed her eyes. 'It's...I feel like pinching myself.' And a couple of tears sparkled on her lashes.

'Briony —— ' he laced his fingers through hers '—can I tell you something? Do you remember the day we landed on the Gordon river?'

Her eyes widened. 'Yes... You were...I couldn't understand your mood, although...' She stopped.

'You did eventually,' he said drily. 'But there was more to it. That beautiful place, St John Falls, reminded me of something—it made me think of the deep, quiet, very heart of our loving. I also had some presentiment that you weren't going to take up my offer and I asked myself why I was the way I was, why I couldn't change, why I had to...cheapen this marvellous thing between us. Unfortunately,' he said very quietly, 'as you know, I didn't change then, but I'd like you to know now that that deep, quiet heart of our loving is something that had never happened to me before, nor will it again except with you.'

She slipped into his arms, her eyes alight with wonder and love, and he caught his breath and buried his face between her breasts.

MILLS & BOON NOW PUBLISH
EIGHT LARGE PRINT TITLES A MONTH.
THESE ARE THE EIGHT NEW TITLES
FOR MAY 1994

———————— * ————————

UNWILLING MISTRESS
by Lindsay Armstrong

ORIGINAL SIN
by Rosalie Ash

ISLAND OF SHELLS
by Grace Green

A TAXING AFFAIR
by Victoria Gordon

WOUNDS OF PASSION
by Charlotte Lamb

SUDDEN FIRE
by Elizabeth Oldfield

LOST IN LOVE
by Michelle Reid

MAKING MAGIC
by Karen Van Der Zee

MILLS & BOON NOW PUBLISH
EIGHT LARGE PRINT TITLES A MONTH.
THESE ARE THE EIGHT NEW TITLES
FOR JUNE 1994

———————— * ————————

BITTER HONEY
by Helen Brooks

THE POWER OF LOVE
by Rosemary Hammond

HEART-THROB FOR HIRE
by Miranda Lee

A SECRET REBELLION
by Anne Mather

THE CRUELLEST LIE
by Susan Napier

THE AWAKENED HEART
by Betty Neels

ITALIAN INVADER
by Jessica Steele

A RECKLESS ATTRACTION
by Kay Thorpe